Locked In

*The Virtual Realms Series:
Book 1*

M. J. Lau

Copyright © 2018 M. J. Lau

All rights reserved.

This is a work of fiction. Names, characters, businesses, events, and incidents are the products of the author's imagination. Any resemblance to actual persons, living or dead, or actual events is purely coincidental (but if some of this stuff happened for real, that would be pretty cool).

DEDICATION

To Andrew, the gaming guru

Cheat Sheet for Noobs

AFK: Away From Keyboard

Buff: a status improvement (like more strength or defense), which usually only lasts for a short time

Loot: Money or gear that players collect after winning in combat or completing a quest

Mob: Non-player creatures in the game that often appear randomly, can be hostile, and which players typically fight to gain XP and/or loot

NPC: Non-Player Characters, often found in towns; they engage in work, dialogue, and commerce with players

OP: Overpowered (opposite of "nerf")

Prestige: A sign of high rank, usually obtained by gaining a lot of experience (XP) or performing difficult achievements

Respawn: to return to your starting (spawn) point after dying in-game

XP: Experience points, which are earned by defeating mobs or other players; the more you have, the better you and your avatar are

CHAPTER 1
BLINK OUT

THE DUNGEONS UNDER SHATTERED PEAK were always dangerous, but they were twice as deadly at night. The pair of one-eyed trolls guarding the entrance propped their bladed clubs on one shoulder, their nine-foot shields obscuring their massive bodies below the chin. Slaying them would only be the beginning; beyond lie flaming skeletons, an army of giant millipedes, Skulklings spitting acid from the ceiling, and of course double the enchanted treasure as during the day. At least, that's what Everstarr was counting on—he'd died twelve times already trying to find out.

From the edge of the Goblin's Forest, the dungeon's entrance looked so close, but Everstarr and his clan members needed a strategic plan to get within range before the trolls spotted them. He was hoping his leader, Lord Baneblade, would somehow turn to him for advice, but even in his mismatched armor, Everstarr didn't stand out.

Lord Baneblade, on the other hand, was impossible to miss. He looked like a steampunk vampire hunter, his blood-red cape and sleek black hair rippling in the steady breeze. The only brightness about him was the two-foot blade strapped to his left arm, gleaming in the moonlight.

After surveying the scene, Baneblade knelt and faced the rest of the group. "All right, men, let's get ready to move out." He fixed his eyes on the two guys next to Everstarr. "KD and Miracle, I want you to pin those trolls down with arrow fire." The elf and the human ranger, respectively, grinned.

His eyes skipped over Everstarr to the next clan member. "Zero, try to blind them with DazzleFlame." The hovering hooded mage nodded.

Baneblade's eyes shifted upward to look at the wall of meat towering above them all. "And Shieldbreaker...do what you do." The whole team laughed as the bearded Viking pumped his fist.

Baneblade's gaze swept over the whole group, yet Everstarr felt like he was still being overlooked. "Everyone else, stay close behind me. Clear?"

A dozen eager warriors grunted their assent. Everstarr cleared his throat and stood, placing himself in Lord Baneblade's line of sight for the first time. "Lord," he squeaked, his high voice clashing with his grizzled, stern face. The others suppressed snorts, but Everstarr pressed on. "Why don't we split into two groups and circle around? A one-eyed troll is a perfect target for a pincer attack."

Baneblade stared hard at Everstarr. He recognized the intensity in the warrior's steel gray eyes. The Lord smiled. "Wolf, Kit, and both Gaijins, go right with Starr. The rest of you follow me." Soon, a lanky spearman, a stealthy cat-girl, and two almost identical samurai joined Everstarr's squad.

Once everyone was in position, Baneblade held up a fist. "On three," he said. "One...two...three!"

A searing green light arced through the air, bursting into blinding flame right in front of the trolls' contorted faces.

The steady thrum of bows sent a storm of arrows raining down on the dazed monsters.

With a primal howl, Shieldbreaker charged, a vee of fighters running at his heels toward the disoriented dungeon guardians. Ten paces from the first troll, he raised his massive battle-axe high. With one heavy stroke, the Viking smashed through the hopeless creature's iron plate mail, leveling it.

"Hold your fire!" Lord Baneblade yelled back to the archers, as the arrows threatened to now rain on their comrades. Everstarr, Wolfgang, and the rest of the fighters swept in from the left of the larger troll after Shieldbreaker slew the first. Suddenly, the DazzleFlame died, and the second troll quickly recovered his sense, bracing himself just in time for Shieldbreaker's next swing.

The shield's metal shrieked, the mighty troll's arm shuddered, and his heels slid back a good yard from the blow. But the axe stopped, protruding four inches through the other side and now stuck fast in the troll's shield. The troll roared, wrenching the shield aside and throwing Shieldbreaker to the ground. He hefted his awful bladed club fifteen feet in the air and brought it down toward the great warrior's skull.

Just then, Wolfgang's halberd slammed into the giant troll's ribcage, jolting it so hard that the shaft snapped and flew from his hands. The monster's downstroke continued, albeit at a different angle, headed now for Shieldbreaker's groin. With a bold leap, Everstarr soared over the Viking's body and slashed through the troll's weapon arm with his Demon Blade, causing both limb and club to spin off into the night. The troll's scream ended as quickly as it began, with Lord Baneblade's arm-sword punching through the creature's throat.

From there, things got crazy.

The next twenty minutes were a free-for-all, with each clan member fighting in their own style as they wove through the snaking dungeon tunnels. They shot and hacked and magicked their way through hordes of goblin priests and giant spiders, healing each other almost constantly.

Everstarr hung with most of the pack until they reached the Mummy's Chambers and everyone had to fend for themselves against the seemingly endless waves of walking corpses. After that, most of the clan headed down the gilded halls to the right of the Dark Sarcophagus, but Everstarr remembered making it this far once before and wanted to try his luck cutting left this time.

"Wolfgang, this way!" he called, waving his best friend over. They scrambled into the dim side corridor just as they heard their clan mates encounter the telltale shrieks of the Skulklings.

Everstarr equipped his Spectral Pendant to illuminate the dark passageway. Even though he was rushing into imminent danger, he couldn't help but admire the attention to detail in the wall carvings and the jeweled ceiling. The richness of the sounds in the hallway put a strange smile on his face as well, the jangle of Wolfgang's beaded necklaces blending with the crunch of their footsteps and the bass of far-off combat shaking the walls.

A faint droning sound grew with each step until Everstarr realized it was the distant roar of a huge fire. He could almost feel the heat on his face as the glow became brighter and brighter.

"Dude, is that what I think it is?" Wolfgang asked, twirling his backup weapon, a Fury Flail, in anticipation.

"It's gotta be," Everstarr replied, swapping out his pendant for a Stone of Protection and lowering his helmet visor.

The two charged into a vast chamber filled with towering shadows dancing in the lights of countless bonfires. They had found a Conference of Mages, which only happens once every 900 Red Moons.

As soon as they entered the massive space, the room erupted in Sorcerer's Lightning and Dragon Breath and Blood of the Ancients. Everstarr and Wolfgang dodged and slashed, zigzagging toward the Eye of Magus at the far end. Smash that and he would capture the whole room.

Everstarr had his sights locked on that iridescent orb, avoiding the crisscrossing spellstorm almost without a thought. The hypnotic colors intensified as he and Wolfgang got closer, and the flashing of the surrounding fires and the bursting of magic all around them only heightened the chaos of light. As they ascended the stairs to the Mage's Altar, Wolfgang raised his flail to strike the Eye as soon as it was in range.

Five paces out, Everstarr stumbled on the steps. His sword arm fell limp at his side. The awful glare of Sorcerer's Vengeance consumed his vision, leaving him in darkness.

CHAPTER 2
IRL

Everett Starner sat up from his bedroom floor. His father came rushing up the stairs two at a time and burst through his bedroom door.

"Ev, what hap—?"

Everett tossed his VR headset on the bed. "I'm fine, Dad. It's over."

His dad checked his pupils and then helped him to his feet. Everett wobbled, so his dad let him sit on the bed. "Take it easy, bud. I'll get your pill."

"I'll come down and get it in a minute, just put it on the counter." His dad hesitated. "I'm fine, Dad, really."

As his father's footsteps receded down the stairs, Everett worked on untangling the wires suctioned to his limbs. The peripherals for *Realms of Glory* were pretty cool, but they weren't without their hang-ups. He loved the responsiveness of the motion sensors and the fidelity of the VR display, but it was hard to forget that you had a two-pound box strapped to the front of your face. When the fighting got intense, you usually ended up wriggling into a snarl of wires at exactly the wrong time. Add to that the joys of light-induced epilepsy and gaming could be a downright suckfest sometimes. Any time he saw flashing lights, he had a chance of—well, what just happened.

After straightening up his gear, Everett grabbed his backpack and rumbled down the stairs.

"Your eggs are by the stove, Ev," his dad called from the hallway. "Watch out for the burner, though, it's still hot."

"Dad! I'm not some helpless little kid who—"

His dad stepped into the doorway to the kitchen, holding the ends of his tie. He arched one eyebrow.

Everett took a breath. "Sorry. I didn't—" He took his plate to the breakfast counter and gathered his thoughts. "I was stupid. I should have avoided the situation, but it just kinda happened. I didn't want to let the guys down." He took his pill and chased it with some OJ.

His dad walked over and gave his neck a reassuring squeeze. "Do you want me to drive you to school today?" He finished tying his tie. "I don't have my first interview until nine."

"Nah," said Everett around a mouthful of eggs. He swallowed. "But, I was hoping Mom could pick me up at the Gamer's Corner this afternoon? I wanted to check out the Interface demo they have on display."

His dad took a sip of some lukewarm coffee and furrowed his brow.

"Didn't you just get that whole virtual reality set-up? I thought that was the best—whatever-ya-call-it."

"Yeah, no, it's really cool, I was just thinking—ya know, maybe at Mom's..."

His dad's face remained relaxed, but Everett knew he struck a nerve. It was better not to say anything else until Dad said something first.

"Well, I can talk to her about it. I mean, you can text her about meeting you there, but the game thing..." His dad's face tried on a stern look, but it never fit right. He added a hand on the shoulder to really sell it. "After this morning, I think we need to have a talk about whether you should be playing games at all."

"That's *why* I want to check out the Interface." Everett took a bite of toast, then gestured with the rest of it. "I wouldn't have to worry about triggering my seizures because I wouldn't be looking at a screen."

"I said I'll talk to your mom about it. Now finish your breakfast, you have like two sec—"

The bus honked outside. Everett shoveled three bites of eggs in his mouth, downed the last of the OJ, and hugged his dad on the way to the door. "Love ya,

Dad— thanks for calling Mom!" he said as he hustled toward the door, not waiting for confirmation.

CHAPTER 3
UNPOPULAR BEFORE IT WAS COOL

The bus ride from Dad's was always the worst—he didn't know anyone, and all the high school kids wanted to do was swear and throw things, mostly in his direction. He just huddled by the window, his backpack blocking off the rest of the seat, while he watched YouTube videos of his favorite *Realms of Glory* players.

Twenty joyous minutes later, Everett disembarked at Howard Taft Junior High. Dozens of kids shoved past him as he made his way toward homeroom.

"You missed some sick loot this morning," Alex said as he sidled up to Everett at his locker. Alex popped off his Beats and tossed his lank black hair out of his eyes. Like his gaming avatar, Alex was tall and lean, but unlike Wolfgang, he rocked some snazzy braces. "Did the bus come early?"

Everett forced a half-smile. "Nah, I had a—I lost my connection. You guys make it out all right?"

"Yeah! I got a sweet Obsidian Spear to replace my busted one. Baneblade ported us back right after we seized all the goods." He winced at his own words. "Sorry."

"What?" Everett shrugged as he closed his locker. "Oh, it's nothin'. C'mon, we'll be late."

They strolled into homeroom and took their adjacent seats. "I just hope I can get us some decent gear before everyone else—"

"Hey, Star-nerd!" Jeff Wenger interrupted, smirking as always. "Did you slay a bunch of Kung Fu gnomes last night? Is your superhero armor fully upgraded?" He leaned on Everett's desk, his meaty freckled face maybe a foot away. Everett didn't have to look behind himself to know that Jeff's buddies, Brayden and Seth, were watching with poorly contained smugness.

Alex clenched his jaw, but Everett just laughed. "Not yet. Did you see the new—"

"Do you meet a lot of babes in your little game world? Any Amazon warriors throwing themselves at your feet?" Jeff laughed at his own wit, straightening up into a wide straddle when Mr. Gemelli came in from the hallway. "Sup, Mr. G?"

"Hey, gang," the teacher replied, doing a cursory

sweep of the room before planting himself at his desk. "Have seat, Mr. Wenger."

"You're gonna wish you had your wonder sword for gym class today," Jeff mumbled to Everett as he walked past him to his seat. His pals snickered and tossed in their own jabs, laced with some profanity.

Everett's face grew hot, but he looked away. Alex sprung up from his seat and charged toward Jeff, even though two desks were in between them. "Say that again and all you'll be able to do is mumble!"

"Mr. Ramirez! Get over here." Mr. Gemelli stood at his desk, all forty-six eyes in the room now on his crimson face. Alex glared at Jeff, who put his hands up in a grand show of shocked innocence. "Now!"

Alex marched to the back of the room, stumbling over Seth's extended foot along the way. Alex took a swat at Seth's binder but failed to knock it on the floor.

"Out in the hall NOW!" The redness on Mr. G's face now encompassed his entire bald head as he flung his arm toward the door. Alex shifted course but took his time to exit. Mr. Gemelli gave everyone a stern look before following Alex out.

The room was silent for the next few seconds, with everyone's eyes shifting toward Jeff's crew. A few girls asked if Jeff and Seth were OK, with the general mood being utter confusion over what set Alex off. Jeff feigned ignorance, his smile as smug as ever.

"Whatever," Brayden said, just loud enough for the whole room to hear. "He thinks he can just go off on people because his dad bailed on him."

Most of the class shook their heads, but not in a pitying way. Everett just seethed, knowing his only ally in the class was in the hall right now.

A few minutes later, the bell mercifully rang, allowing Everett to gather up his belongings and the last shreds of his dignity before heading to first period. Gym.

Jeff matched his pace to walk out of the room at just the same time. "You won't always have your boyfriend to stand up for you," he muttered in Everett's ear, then shouldered past him to catch up with his cronies.

After homeroom it was gym, which was basically as terrible as he expected it to be. Jeff didn't get to harass him too much during floor hockey, but once they were in the locker room, Everett's sneakers became the focus of a very one-sided game of hot potato.

Math was OK. Everett was pretty good with numbers, but not quite good enough to ever actually get noticed as being any good. He sat in the back, got everything right, and took a sliver of solace from the fact that he was totally invisible.

In Spanish he was feeling so much better, he

raised his hand to answer a question for the first time all year. In his enthusiasm, he completely mangled the pronunciation of *rápidamente*, making his first act of participation also his last.

Science was the usual forty-minute notes sesh. It wasn't too terrible, though, because his crush sat at his table, and she didn't even cringe when he smiled at her today.

At lunch he ate alone because Alex had to spend the rest of the day in the office. Everett just gnawed on some pizza sticks and watched videos about the Interface to pass the time. Nobody could actually record in-game content since it transmits the game directly into your head, but the interviews with people who used it made him even more eager to try the Interface out after school.

By early afternoon, the drama from homeroom was dust in the rearview. English and social studies were a blur—he was busy watching the clock. Two hours to Interface.

Ninety minutes.

Forty-five.

CHAPTER 4
THE INTERFACE

Everett had just finished his five-minute demo—there was a line out the door, so they kept everyone moving—when his mom came into Gamer's Corner. She was smiling just enough to make it clear she was happy to see him, but not so happy that she'd be reaching for her wallet any time soon. Everett was expecting to make a sales pitch, so the forty-minute wait before his demo gave him a chance to polish up his lines.

She must have come straight from a showing—she still had her Realtor lanyard on. "Are you ready?" she said, looking toward the door.

Everett gestured toward the sleek metallic headset, currently wrapped around the shaggy haircut of a gangly, tattooed skater. "Don't you want to see it? You're already here…"

"You can tell me all about it in the car." His mom

put her hand on his back, giving the same forced smile to everyone they passed in the store on the way out. He knew it wouldn't be easy to win her over, and leaving the store this way felt like a defeat, but if he played his cards right, maybe waiting until they were home would make the convincing go smoother.

The whole ride home, Everett refrained from even talking about the Interface. He indulged his mom with genuine insight about school—even played up the "highlights" for her rather than going monosyllabic with all his answers.

When they ate dinner, he didn't mention it once. Mom talked about the open houses she had this weekend, and you would think Everett was actually interested in buying the properties based on his active listening skills.

As he helped clean the dishes, he was all business. He scrubbed the pans without being asked, and when his mom thanked him for hand-drying everything, he deflected by expressing gratitude for a delicious meal.

It wasn't until he was working on his homework that he even broached the subject, and he let his mom say her piece without interruption. It seemed like she had done some research on the whole thing, but she was still a little over-the-top with her concerns.

"C'mon, Mom, it's not the Matrix."

"You're plugging a cord into the back of your

head—"

"Side of my head."

"Side of your head, and it tricks your mind into seeing a different world."

"And hearing and feeling it, yes."

She gave him a look. "You're not helping your case."

Everett took a deep breath. "Mom, it's like reading a good book. You picture it all in your head. You imagine what it feels like to be the characters, but you're still in the real world. It's immersive, but it doesn't replace my reality." He had heard that from a YouTuber he followed and delivered the lines convincingly. "I'm still able to see what's around me. I can hear you if you need me. If I need to use the bathroom—"

"All right, I get the idea. But something in your brain? Especially with your condition—"

"That's actually what makes it a good idea," he said, trying not to rush this next argument. He knew this was his best shot, so he tried to keep cool. "TV screens and VR displays flash lights in my eyes—and that can trigger my epilepsy. The Interface bypasses my eyes and just puts the picture in my head, right in front of my mind's eye. It's the safest way for me to play."

She hesitated for a moment, and he somehow managed to keep his heart from leaping out of his chest. "I just don't get how they do this without a doctor. I mean, is that shady kid at the game store just going to jab some metal into your brain—"

He couldn't help but laugh at that one. "It's not an implant, Mom, it just wraps around the back of my head. I would take it off when I'm not playing. It's basically wifi, but it transmits brainwaves." He didn't mention that it essentially hijacks your occipital lobe—your vision centers—and even influences your amygdala to make you feel things—like emotions, not just sensations. Moms don't need to know *everything*.

His mom made a noncommittal grunt. "I'll think about it." His mom's phone buzzed, and she thumbed through the message.

Everett tried to stay chill, but his insides were on parade. For most moms, "I'll think about it" was just a nice "no"; for his mom, that was about as close to an agreement as he could have hoped for. "OK, cool—so, does that mean like by this weekend...?"

His mom was mid-message, and almost flung her phone when he interrupted. "Everett, I said I'll think about it! This is a big decision, and I'm not made of money!"

His brain knew he pushed his luck, but that did nothing to insulate his heart. "Jeez, OK, sorry for asking..."

She slouched and sighed. "Everett, honey, c'mon—I didn't mean to—"

But he was already down the hall, taking the stairs two at a time up to his room.

CHAPTER 5
THE SCORE

When Everstarr awoke at the inn, he made his way down to the warehouse to pick through the remaining loot from that morning. All the top-tier weapons would probably be claimed, but maybe someone overlooked a useful accessory or left behind some decent armor when they found some higher-quality stuff.

When he got there, he caught a reflection of himself in a giant Mirror Shield; Everett might be a shrimpy little nerd with bad posture, but Everstarr loomed broad and tall in his glistening armor, like Sir Lancelot if he were played by The Rock.

Standing a little taller now, Everstarr swaggered by swarms of clan members milling about, chatting and showing off their newest kit. ØGravityØ was combing through tomes of spells, practicing one incantation after another. KD tested a vapor bow and some fanged arrows, shredding a target dummy along the far wall. A few Lords stood near the main pile, monitoring the noobs so they couldn't run off with anything OP.

Everstarr spotted Wolfgang in a corner by some promising gear and sauntered over.

"Wow, there's still this much left?" Everstarr said, examining some onyx plate mail and frost amulets.

"You should have seen it this morning," Wolfgang replied, clad head to toe in matching dragon scale armor. "It had to be the haul of the year!"

"Do you think other clans heard about it?"

"They had to," Wolfgang said. "Any time an Eye gets smashed, everyone in-game gets a banner notification. The LORDZ must be top of the hit list now." He flexed comically, but there was a little quaver in his voice that Everstarr could empathize with all too well. Even with awesome equipment, their clan was still no match for the bigger, more experienced crews.

Everstarr surveyed the sprawling area. "So the Lords aren't just here to babysit the low-levs...they're bracing for an attack." He froze for a moment.

Wolfgang waved his arms around to get Everstarr's attention. "Yo, Ev. You AFK?"

"No, I'm here," he replied. "And so is most of our clan. So if someone tried to raid us right now..."

"They'd wipe out most of our leaders, plus get all

our stuff!"

"We gotta scatter!" Everstarr rushed toward Lords Baneblade, Forlani, and Celt. He sketched a bow and addressed them just as turned to face him. "Everybody needs to fill their inventory and get out of here. If anyone raids us, we'll be too spread out for them to get much."

The Lords consulted off-mic. Everstarr exchanged a look and a shrug with Wolfgang. Lord Forlani, the tallest Lord by a good foot, aimed his long, pinched face down at Everstarr. Then he put a hand on the young man's shoulder and curled his thin lips into a smile. "Lordz Clan, all ears," he broadcasted over ClanChat. "Fill all empty slots at the warehouse and stash the excess in different spots throughout town—the more random, the better." He then turned and addressed only Everstarr and the other Lords. "Once you've secured your loot, rally your best troops at the walls to fortify."

He broadcasted to the clan one last time: "Everyone, go!"

The warehouse burst into a hive of activity, with mounds of gear vanishing as dozens of clan members maxed out their inventories. Zero zapped piles of loot off to who knows where. Everstarr and Wolfgang snatched up some top-shelf equipment and raced out the back door.

"Meet me at the south wall in five!" Everstarr

called over his shoulder as he headed east and Wolfgang went west.

Even though they were soon on opposite sides of town, Wolfgang was still loud in Everett's ear, speaking in giddy fragments about pulling this off. Everstarr dumped his excess inventory in a trapped lockbox behind the bakery, then scrambled toward the south gate. Wolfgang assured him he'd beat him there.

Just as the twin south towers came into sight, Everstarr's chest throbbed from the bass of several explosions. Voices erupted in his ear. Pandemonium swept across ClanChat, but it wasn't coming from the southern wall. It was from the North.

CHAPTER 6
SLAYYY

The south side of Lordz Landing faced a rolling landscape, dotted with clusters of trees and hemmed in by the Frostfang Peaks. It wasn't ideal terrain to invade from, but it was the only side that it made any sense to approach from. The western wall faced a steep hill with no cover, and the east side was too rocky to advance over with horses or anything with wheels. The north side of town bordered a steep cliff, which dropped a hundred feet down to the Restless Sea. They had a wall there, but it was rudimentary and thinly manned. No one would attack from that side—how could they?

"Get to the Square!" Lord Forlani commanded over ClanChat. "Bleak Clan raiders!"

Everstarr wheeled around and charged north, weaving down alleys toward the Square. When he rounded the corner of the inn, he saw the warehouse was already engulfed in flames. Enraged Bleakers streamed out into the Square, fanning out into the surrounding area. Everstarr couldn't help but smile at their frustration, but his joy was short-lived. The town's NPCs were running around frantically, some getting captured, others slain. They weren't real people, but they were familiar faces and they kept the town running, so their suffering, as it were, made him a little heartsick.

The Bleakers began wrecking key buildings around the Square—the treasury, the guild hall, the market. They couldn't damage the inn or the Lords' manors because characters always need somewhere to respawn, but the Bleak Clan members broke inside and camped on the beds so anyone they killed couldn't come back until they left.

Wolfgang came to Everstarr's side just as the last of the Bleakers emptied out of the warehouse. A single figure strode out into the slanting sunlight. "Where are all the fighters in this town?" the dark-haired assassin bellowed. He was compact, wiry, with a short curved blade and a crooked smile. To the average person, he was just some scraggly kid, but the sight of him made Everstarr's heart leap into his throat.

"Jake da Rippa," Wolfgang said, his awe coming through even in his hateful tone. Jake was a legend, one of the highest ranked players in the game, with over 500 clan-leader kills. Even the biggest clans—SpiderGods, RoME, Blood Brothers, KJZ Pagans—steered clear of Bleak Clan because of Jake.

Apparently unaware of—or unfazed by—Jake's reputation, Shieldbreaker responded to the challenge. He raised his shiny new Mythril battle-axe and bore down on Jake with an ogre-horn shield.

"Ooh, a big boy!" Jake braced himself. "I haven't killed a Viking in a long time!"

As fast as Shieldbreaker was, Jake's speed was astonishing. Everstarr could barely distinguish Jake's deft feint, parry, sidestep, and counter; Shieldbreaker was on the ground faster than he could fall. The Viking's battle-axe flew from his hand across the cobblestones of the Square. then Jake let out a sick cackle, stepped on his back, and spun his sword.

"No!" Wolfgang cried, knowing what was next: an execution.

Dying in-game was bad enough—you lost some loot, your respawn was delayed, and sometimes you even lost XP—but executions were much worse and mercifully rare. They required a flawless defeat, exquisite timing, and frankly a total lack of respect for your opponent. Executions ended a character for good—no respawn, no loot, you couldn't even reuse your name. You had to start the game over from the beginning. Rebuilding what you had could take months.

Wolfgang lunged forward to avenge their fallen friend, but Everstarr held him back. "Not now," he rasped. "We have to stop this raid or we'll lose the whole town." Lords Forlani and Celt rallied forces near the east edge of the Square and managed to slow the Bleakers' advance.

Everstarr gestured with a tilt of his head. "C'mon." He led Wolfgang toward a side street on the south side.

"Why are we running from the battle? We have to stop them!"

"Exactly—and that's going to take a Miracle."

CHAPTER 7
RAIN

As he approached the western wall, Everstarr saw two elves on the parapet, picking off Bleakers that straggled into that end of town.

"KD! Miracle!" He jumped from a nearby balcony to reach the top of the wall, followed closely by Wolfgang.

The archers didn't stop firing arrows, but Miracle-Man, the dark elf, at least tilted his head toward them. "Yo, you here to help?"

"Actually, we need your help...can you two volley shots into the Square from here?"

The dark elf seemed to dance in place a little, angling his bow up and down. "I'd have to move to that tower, then yeah." He indicated a turret about eighty yards away along the outer wall.

"OK. Can you two get there and start raining arrows down on the Square on my signal? Start at the southern end and sweep northward, all right?" They nodded and started making their way toward the tower.

Everstarr went to hurry away but turned back. "Hey, you guys seen Zero?"

KD, who was strafing and firing as he headed toward the tower, called back. "Over on the east side with the Lords, I think!"

Everett gave a quick salute and rushed after Wolfgang. They leaped off the wall and circled around to the east side, avoiding Bleakers as much as possible. It took a few minutes to weave their way across town, and as they went, Everstarr rallied some of the low-levs and gave them positions to guard a few blocks south of the Square. Fewer and fewer clan members were around because the Bleakers were still camping on a lot of the respawn points, but most of the heavy hitters were hanging in.

Green and red light flashed on the sides of buildings to Everstarr's left. ØGravityØ was close. "Zero!" he hailed over ClanChat. "Can you fall back to the stables? Wolfgang and I have a plan!"

A few more flares of light bounced off the alley walls, and then ØGravityØ sailed toward them, hovering a foot off the ground as always. If that wasn't cool enough, Zero also never spoke. "The magic does the talking," Lord Baneblade would always say with pride.

"Zero, we are getting more outnumbered by the minute. We have to drive these guys out of town and put up a peace shield before they wreck all our key buildings."

"Or execute our best guys," Wolfgang chimed in bitterly.

Everett couldn't argue with that, so he pressed on. "We're going to funnel the Bleakers into the Square and hopefully push them back into the sea. Can you drive them toward the center of town so we can concentrate our attacks and force a retreat?"

ØGravityØ hovered in front of them for a moment, eyes aglow beneath a heavy hood. Wolfgang suddenly took on a golden aura, and Everstarr also had a protection buff now. Then Zero vanished in a cloud of purple smoke.

Wolfgang turned to Everstarr and shrugged. "I'll take that as a *yes*?"

Moments later, the sky began to darken, and heavy red clouds coalesced around the perimeter of the town. Thunder rolled, and bio-flame began to rain down, slowly at first, but with greater intensity as the ring of clouds contracted. The liquid rained from the sky like water, but when it hit anything living, it stuck and caught fire like napalm.

Wanting a better view, Wolfgang did some parkour to reach a nearby rooftop, and Everstarr struggled to keep up.

"Dude, do you still not have the Interface?" Wolfgang asked once Everstarr caught up. "You have no idea what you're missing. It's so responsive—I think of a move and I'm doing it. And the graphics! I can't even call them graphics, because they're what you actually see in your head, but like—"

"Could we not do this right now?" Everstarr said, shaking his head and smiling. He pointed to the street below. They saw raiders running for the middle of town, some on fire. "C'mon, I don't know how long this'll last!"

They raced toward the inn, unconcerned about Bleakers now that they were mostly running for their lives. The campers inside the inn seemed unnerved by their teammates panicking, which made them easy pickings for Everstarr and Wolfgang. Wolfgang was able to one-tap many of the mid-level Bleakers thanks to his new halberd, and Everstarr drove at least ten into the streets without taking much damage at all.

With each bed they cleared, another teammate respawned, and although they were eager to chase their routed opponents, Everstarr called them back. "You don't want to go out there," he assured them. "It's raining pretty bad."

At that, he gave the order for KD and Miracle to start firing arrows. From the inn window, Everstarr could see Bleakers dropping under the missile fire, although Jake and most of his upper echelon took very little damage due to their obscenely high prestige levels.

"Back in the boats!" Jake shouted, waving his clan toward the hole in the north wall.

Lords Baneblade, Forlani, and Celt pushed a column of stubborn raiders out of the east end. Zero's rain had petered off already, but some of the noobs managed to chase out the Bleakers from the south side. Everstarr told the archers to hold their fire—the new arrows they were using did splash damage, so even friendlies could be hurt.

When the archers let up, the retreating Bleakers quickly turned on their pursuers and forced them back. Wolfgang, who leaned in the doorway of the inn with a satisfied grin, straightened up and grew tense. Before he could voice his protest, Everstarr shoved past him, bolting top speed at the melee with his sword drawn.

"Ev, wait up!"

By the time Wolfgang got out of the doorway, Everstarr had charged his dash attack and leveled two Bleakers with his shoulder. He combo-ed into a whirling sword attack, sending three more onto their backs.

The noobs, previously frightened by the sudden retaliation of the Bleakers, now directed their terror toward the ferocity of their clan member. They continued to stagger back, even though Everstarr was crossing swords with the only Bleaker still standing before them, and the Bleaker was getting the worst of it.

Wolfgang reached the scene only a few seconds later, but he was already too late. The bodies of the fallen Bleakers began to fade away, and Everstarr had just bashed the helmet off the last one standing. Wolfgang stood off to the side with the cowering noobs, smirking. "Watch this—he's gonna wreck this clown!"

Everstarr cocked his sword back to finish off the dazed Bleaker, but he stopped himself mid-swing. His usual fluidity turned into a strange series of movements, puzzling those around him.

Wolfgang's smile faded and his brow furrowed. "Ev, what's wrong?" Without the Interface, Everett's facial expressions didn't reflect his true feelings. But when Wolfgang's eyes flicked over to the dazed Bleaker, it all crystallized.

The Bleaker looked just like Jeff.

Faster than Wolfgang could even think, Everstarr lunged at the raider, smashing the hilt of his sword into the man's mouth. He continued to rain blows on the helpless figure, slashing at his arms and chest even after he collapsed to the ground. Everstarr knelt over him, screaming with rage as he pounded the man's face, and eventually the cobblestones beneath when the body faded away.

As Everstarr knelt there, wracked with anguish, no one around him moved. No one except the Bleaker behind him, a disheveled buccaneer who wasn't quite dead from the initial charge. The pirate sprung to his feet and made for Everstarr's back.

"Noooo!" Wolfgang closed the distance between himself and the would-be assassin in a blur, his new spear cleaving the air with impossible speed. It skewered the Bleaker's skull as if it were piercing a melon.

The impact of the blow and the Bleaker falling next to him jarred Everett out of his crazed state. Startled, he jumped back to his feet and seemed to notice Wolfgang and the noobs for the first time. Their alarmed expressions unnerved him, but that was no match for the fear roiling inside him.

A notification appeared in the upper left corner of Everstarr's field of vision. Wolfgang just executed one of the top Bleakers, earning him a Headhunter's Badge. A red drop of blood—a Revenge marker—now hovered over Wolfgang's head.

He was now a marked man for the entire Bleak Clan.

CHAPTER 8
RANK UP

As the last of the remaining Bleakers slid down the cliff face to the galleons waiting below, Lord Celt erected a peace shield and everyone took a collective sigh of relief. The survivors—and the respawns as they popped back in—gathered in the Square to assess the damage.

The town was a wreck. Every optional facility was demolished: the forge, the warehouse, the market, the stables. The treasury was nearly emptied out. The Lords' homes were still standing but had been sacked. Most characters now had their spawn points set to the inn because over half the houses were destroyed. It was, in a word, "suckish."

Lord Celt raised his hand to quiet the crowd. He wore only light leather and chain mail, but his burly frame and mane of red hair made him look twice as tough as the other Lords. All eyes were on him in seconds. "We obviously got hit hard by the Bleak Clan. It will take us a few days—real-time—to fix all this. The Lords will each take a section of town and assign people to rebuild. We should be good with peace shields until the important stuff is back up, starting with our walls.

"But even after that, we need to keep our guard up," he continued, now looking in Wolfgang's direction, "and not look for more trouble. We didn't just lose buildings and loot today...we lost some clanmates." He held up Shieldbreaker's axe, sending murmurs through the crowd.

"Still, we have much to take pride in," Lord Forlani said, stepping forward. "Nearly all of our best equipment was untouched, thanks to the quick efforts to stash our valuables throughout town. We even gained some epic gear from the Bleakers who fell today." He held up a horrifyingly awesome-looking spear and gestured toward the other Lords, who held triblades and spiked mauls and assorted pieces of armor that looked custom-made. This caused the mumblings of the clan to shift from the minor to the major key.

"So let us begin rebuilding," Lord Baneblade announced over the excitement. "We have proven ourselves a mighty clan today, and this was not the last time others will seek to challenge our greatness. Our power comes not from the weapons in our hands, but the way we wield them. We fight best when we fight together.

"And one clanmate in particular has shown great bravery and innovation in leading our clan toward higher levels." Here his tone shifted from the formal to the familial. The clan members murmured and nodded in agreement, but Everstarr looked around, confused. Then it hit him—they were all looking at the same guy. Him.

Lord Baneblade advanced toward Everstarr, and the other lords followed. Clearly this was a positive situation, but Everstarr's stomach grew hotter as they came closer and closer. He tried to cover his nerves with a smile, but then silently cursed himself—they wouldn't be able to see that.

Lord Baneblade stopped a few paces in front of him and unsheathed his legendary claymore. "Please kneel, Everstarr." Everstarr complied, looking at the ground. There was total silence as the Lord's blade hovered over his left shoulder, then his right. "And rise, Lord Starr, Defender of the West."

Everstarr stood and looked out at the entire clan staring back at him. He couldn't believe this was really happening, but his banner notifications confirmed everything: "Player Everstarr is now Lord Starr of Lordz Clan," "Lord Starr gifted 100,000 EXP from Lord Baneblade—Prestige Level 10," "Received +10 Gungnir (Imbued Lightning)".

The clan erupted with cheers, and Wolfgang looked over at him, smiling wide enough for the both of them.

CHAPTER 9
GAME DAY

Most of the week was pretty forgettable—school, home, sleep—but Everett was excited to head off to Mom's for the weekend. Mom never planned trips anywhere or made him go to visit boring relatives he barely knew. He wouldn't be able to hang out with Alex next door, but he could game with him all day long online. He even managed to bring his new VR setup from Dad's; his mom was kinda weird about it at first, but eventually was like, "Ok, but don't make a habit of it."

So when Everett woke up Saturday super early—9 AM—he raced downstairs to grab a quick breakfast before his day of gaming could begin. As he stood impatiently by the toaster waiting to snatch his waffle midair, he thumbed through his Snap-Chats, vainly hoping that messages would appear.

From upstairs, his mom's footsteps rumbled through the ceiling, then clopped down the steps.

"What do you mean you can't—Yeah? Well, who's this 'friend' that you're—No, you don't get to—UGH!" She slammed her phone down on the counter, then jumped when she saw Everett standing right next to her.

Everett leaned back, his eyes wide. "Mom, what's wrong?" His mom was way too dressed up for a morning of cleaning the bathrooms. He had a momentary panic attack that it was actually Sunday and they had to go to church. Then he saw some flyers in her hand. "I thought you didn't have to work today?"

"I picked up a client from Bev because they could only look at places today, and she was busy with an open house." She searched the junk basket for her keys, then spotted them by the coffee maker.

"Oh, well, that's good, right? You get paid for those, don't you?" Everett retrieved his waffle and took a huge bite.

"Only if I sell the house." She inspected her phone to see if it was still functional. "I tried to get your dad to come get you, but he's 'busy helping a friend move.' Since when did your dad have friends?"

Everett held up both hands and looked away. He knew better than to get involved in any of that.

His mom began digging through her purse. "Well, someone needs to be here with you before I go. Maybe I can drop you off at Grandma's on the way..."

Grandma didn't even have wifi, let alone a VR-ready console. He'd miss out on half a day of gaming, minimum. "I don't need to go to Grandma's if you're just leaving for an hour or two—I'm 14!"

"After what happened at your dad's the other day, I'm not leaving you here alone."

"Mom, I'm fine, I'll be fine. Look!" He rattled an anti-seizure pill from his bottle and swallowed it. "Nothing to worry about."

His mom narrowed her eyes. "Why are you so dead-set on staying home? What are you planning to do?"

"Nothing! I just don't want to go to Grandma's, or Dad's, or anywhere else."

She took his face in her hands, her eyes filling with concern. "Everett, honey—did something happen at your father's? I won't be angry, I just want to know..."

He pulled away, throwing his hand up. "No, mom, jeez! I just don't want to spend half the day going back and forth in a car. I can stay here, I have my phone. I won't even leave my room."

His mom cocked her jaw, weighing her options before responding. Then her phone rang. "Shoot! They're already at the house." Her hands waggled by her head as if she were shaking a helmet. "Fine, you can stay home alone, just—GAH!" Her phone chimed again.

She threw her phone in her purse and shuffled

toward the door. "You can stay home, but I am going to ask Mrs. Lentz to check in on you in an hour—" The heel of her shoe snapped off, sending her stumbling into the hallway.

Everett caught her by the shoulder before she ate the linoleum. Her purse flung loose and vomited its contents across the foyer. Her face went from red to almost purplish in about two seconds.

Everett guided her to the steps and faced her. "Mom, take a breath. I'll clean this up." He gathered scattered items and shoveled them into his mom's purse. "Are you OK? Did you hurt your ankle or anything?"

His mom buried her face in her hands, elbows on knees, knees together, feet far apart. He couldn't tell if she was angry, sad, or embarrassed, but he was guessing all three emotions were mixed in there somewhere.

He handed her the purse. "Mom, I'm sorry I got upset. I'm not mad at you, I just don't want to go anywhere—"

His mom wiped her face and sniffled, pulling off a smile. "No, I know, I just—I want to make sure you're OK, all right? Some days I just feel like I make all the wrong decisions for you, and I worry—" Her phone buzzed from the depths of her purse. "Seriously?" She growled and laughed.

Everett laughed with her. "You're awesome,

Mom." He stood, offering to help her up. "C'mon, how can I help?"

His mom stood and gathered herself, flouncing her hair. "Run upstairs and get my red pumps? They're in my closet."

"Pumps?"

"My red heels." He gave her a blank look. "Shoes, my red high-heel shoes."

"Um, OK. Be right back." He jogged up the steps.

He pushed the door open to his mom's room, trying to ignore the weird feeling he got whenever he set foot in there. It was a big, clean, nicely decorated room that always smelled like her perfume, but it creeped him out nonetheless.

He had to cross to the far side, around the bed, to get to her closet. He opened the door and swiped at the air a few times until he caught and yanked the string for the light. The usual sight of a thousand dresses surrounded him, plus the shelves were lined with all kinds of musty old boxes, photo albums, and fancy hats sitting on Styrofoam heads, adding to his overall awkward feeling.

Everett then realized he should probably look down if he was going to find the shoes his mom wanted. That's when he saw something very unusual indeed, boxed up in the back corner. Oh, he'd seen it before, many times—*dreamed* about it, in fact. He just never thought he'd see it here, on his mom's closet floor.

The Interface.

A minute later, Everett galloped down the stairs two at a time, managing somehow to keep his face from betraying the utter exuberance in his soul. "Here you go," he said, almost nonchalantly, when he handed his mom her shoes.

"Thanks, sweetie," his mom chirped, kicking off her broken shoes and putting on the new ones.

As his mom backed out of the driveway, Everett stood in the doorway waving goodbye, smiling so wide it almost hurt.

CHAPTER 10
GET REAL

The first time Everett used the Interface—really used it, not just doing the clunky demo at Gamer's Corner—was unreal. It was like breathing underwater or flying through space: amazing to imagine, but seemingly impossible.

It didn't *look* like he was playing the best game ever. It was like he was living the most exciting dream of his life. The morning breeze blew through the vents in his helmet. His armor hung heavy on his shoulders and chest, and the weathered grip of his sword chafed his hand. His feet actually ached in his bulky metallic boots.

The graphics—no, the actual sights he was seeing—were crisp and detailed no matter how close he looked at his shield or the ground or the frame of the tavern going up beside the inn. Everything was clear as day from the Square to the edge of town, past the walls, to the rolling hills and mountains to the south, which looked bluer as they got closer to the horizon.

"Everstarr—Lord Starr, are you all right?" Kit stood a few yards off, looking at him askance.

"What? Oh, yeah, I'm fine."

Kit smiled, her purple cat-eyes twinkling. "You just got the Interface, didn't you?"

Lord Starr laughed. "How could you tell?"

"Well, for one, you have actual facial expressions, not just the stock look you had before." She moved toward him, casually twirling a dagger. "Plus, you haven't moved in like five minutes other than to look around like a star-struck newborn." She took him by the hand. "Wanna see what it can really do?"

For the next two hours—in real life, two days in game time—Lord Starr and Kit toured the city, explored the landscape around Lordz Landing, and learned how to interact with every object and person in-game with greater depth and nuance than he had ever imagined possible.

He tasted a sugarfruit fresh from the trees on Fern's Hill, savoring the juices as they ran down his chin.

He caught frogs in the stream by the mill, stroking their slippery skin.

He carved his initials into the ornate doorway of

his Lord's Manor on the Square.

He talked at length with the new NPCs—not just the stock "Hello, [insert name], how may I help thee?", but real conversations about the town, their work, their families and lives. Everett knew it was all fake, dialogue retrieved from servers in who-knows-where, but it was as real to him as talking to his friends at school. *Or, ya know, the kids at school who would be my friends, if I had any.*

Once he finally got used to being Lord Starr-ed every few minutes, he figured he should get to work doing Lord things, namely getting his new section of town back in shape. He walked over to the west end of Lordz Landing. He summoned all the NPCs and active players in the area to the big fountain, one of the only remaining landmarks.

He surveyed the desolation and the subdued but hopeful faces of those around him before speaking. "Citizens of Lordz Landing, it is with a heavy heart that I address you for the first time as the Lord of the West," he began, his voice taking on a ringing authority that surprised even him. "An awful enemy attacked us, jealous of our greatness. Our homes have been damaged, our valuables plundered, and many of those dear to us...are no longer here."

He saw some of those around him shifting awkwardly, and he figured his nervousness was contagious. He paused a moment, deciding to drop the act. "I'm no Lord. Most of you just know me as Everstarr. I'm a kid who just really likes this game, and I've come to love hanging out with all of you here. I want to put everything back to the way it was, but obviously I can't do that. So," he said, sighing.

"The first thing I want us to do is get everyone's house restored. Waking up to that wallpaper in the inn makes me want to gouge my eyes out." That remark earned him some laughs.

He shifted back to a more serious tone: "There are some guys working on my Lord's Manor in the Square, but that's hardly a priority; I'll send them here to help you guys rebuild faster.

"Secondly, I want our defenses reinforced and a steady rotation of guards on the walls and in the towers to prevent any more sneak attacks. We can't afford to wait for trouble to ride up before we react." The crowd murmured their assent heartily.

"Last of all, but perhaps most importantly," he said, his eyes and voice gaining intensity, "I want this fountain destroyed."

The active players began griping but quickly checked themselves as soon as they remembered Everstarr was a Lord now.

A hint of a smile crept across Lord Starr's face. "I want it replaced with a greater fountain, with a huge memorial statue in the center, dedicated to the original champion of the West...Shieldbreaker."

The small gathering nearly burst with resounding approval, and that filled him with an emotion that the Interface couldn't entirely take credit for.

CHAPTER 11
THE GENERAL

After a break to eat lunch, rush through some homework, and text a bit his mom (she would be another hour at least!), Everett was back in-game to check on the construction projects in his end of town. Most of the houses were back to normal, and the walls were getting reinforced ahead of schedule. He worked closely on the Shieldbreaker Memorial with the NPC masons and Kit, who had surprising design skills. *She was surprising in many ways*, Lord Starr admitted with a grin.

A chime notified him that Wolfgang was now playing, and sure enough, his hunched form trotted over from the direction of the inn about a minute later. He slowed down as he approached Lord Starr, leaning to one side with a sly smile.

"You got it!" He looked Lord Starr over. "You're plugged in now!"

"Yeah, I—well, my mom bought it, but she doesn't know I found it yet," he said with a laugh.

Wolfgang took in the area with a sweeping gaze. "It's looking good, boss man! So, where's my mansion?"

Lord Starr pointed at the ruins of the bakery. "I saved that spot for you."

"Oh, wow," Wolfgang said, pushing Lord Starr's shoulder, "I see it really pays to have connections in this town."

"JK," Lord Starr replied, walking down the road slightly to get a better look at the main intersection. He aimed a hand eastward. "I have some NPCs setting you up on that far corner, overlooking the new monument we're putting in."

Wolfgang laughed. "You're a Lord for five minutes and you're already building statues of yourself? Dude, the power's gone straight to your head."

"It's for Shieldbreaker." Wolfgang turned toward the voice just in time to see Kit walk over and sidle up to Everett. She pointed toward Wolfgang's new place. "You'll have the best view in town."

Wolfgang leaned back and shifted his eyes between Kit and Lord Starr. "Oh...oh, I see. So this is a thing. Behold the power of the Interface!"

Kit and Lord Starr both tried to raise objections, but Wolfgang was already off to scope out his new digs and instruct the NPCs to add more trap doors.

"Ignore him," Everett said, waving Wolfgang off, "he's just jealous."

"Of you or me?" Kit joked.

As they had a laugh, one of the Gaijin (Everett could never tell the two apart) rushed over to them. "Lord Starr! Lord Starr!" He stopped to catch his breath. "RoME clan is approaching from the southwest! They're about a mile out and marching fast."

Everett knew the Interface was lifelike, but he doubted that it accurately conveyed the sight of his eyes bugging out of his head at this news. "Seriously? How many?" He tried but failed to sound calm.

"Maybe fifty..."

A slight wave of relief washed over him. "OK, so not a full raiding party."

"Yeah," Gaijin Ichi said, still wide-eyed, "but General Sulla is leading them."

Inside, Everett wanted to release a prolonged string of profanity, but outwardly he was composed. "OK. I'll notify the other Lords. Send the archers to their positions on the walls, at the ready. Do NOT let them fire until I give them the order."

Gaijin Ichi nodded and raced back toward the perimeter, waving people along as he went. Everett sent alerts to the other Lords, assuring them he had it under control.

Kit was biting her lip when Lord Starr turned back around, but she tried to look hopeful. "I could slip over the wall and scout them out from the Hillside Forest, maybe draw some of them away from town—"

Lord Starr held up his hands. "No, it's not worth the risk. We have a peace shield up, so going out there just puts you in danger. They aren't planning to attack right now, and they didn't bring the numbers to indicate a full-on invasion. So…"

"So maybe they just want to talk?"

"Maybe. But about what?"

Kit just shrugged. Eventually, their curiosity overtook their caution, and the two of them made for the southern gate.

Once there, Lord Starr convinced the guards on duty to lower the drawbridge—"I promise, it won't deactivate the peace shield"—and looked out the southern gate. In the distance, three score RoME clan members stood in a semicircle, gathered just outside of arrow range in the rocky swale due south of their town.

Everett had never encountered any of them before, but their reputations preceded them. Many of their gamertags had golden emblems beside them—signs that they have been playing *Realms of Glory* since it began, and had attained Elite Prestige ranking. His stomach turned like a washing machine. When the portcullis ratcheted open, snowing down flecks of rust that failed to impress Everett with their realism at that particular moment, he steeled himself and walked out to start the parlay.

"Hail, RoME clan!" Lord Starr raised a hand in greeting. The RoMANS remained in a loose circle, apparently deep in discussion.

Maybe they didn't hear me, Everett thought, continuing to advance. Once he halved the distance between them, he tried again, at twice the volume: "RoME clan, I am Lord Starr of—"

The RoME clan abruptly stopped talking and turned to stare at the screaming guy walking toward them. The circle then divided in two, making way for a towering figure to come forward. He held up a hand as much in greeting as to halt Everett's loud and lengthy introduction.

"Lord Starr, yes, a pleasure to meet you," the brawny man in gleaming armor said, his voice calm but full of authority. He wore heavy plate mail, with elaborate metalwork and gold etching all over, and a long red cape flapped in the breeze behind him. The only part of him not laden with steel was his head, which had the effect of making him look both more human and also inhumanly brave at the same time. "On behalf of RoME clan, I am here to make an offer. Might I confer with the full leadership of Lordz clan regarding this matter?"

Lord Starr stopped in his tracks and tried on his best smile. "Of course, General Sulla," he said, his voice catching in his throat. "Please, right this way."

The massive man, looking about forty but still built like a soldier, took a step forward and put a meaty hand on Lord Starr's shoulder. "I'd be happy to follow you," he said, turning Starr toward the town and pointing at the ramparts, "once you tell your archers to lower their bows."

Everett's neck and ears grew very hot. "Definitely, yeah," he stammered. He notified the other Lords of General Sulla's request and ordered the archers to stand down.

Satisfied, The General gestured toward Lordz Landing. "Lead the way."

CHAPTER 12
THE DEAL

This is insane. The General? Right next to me? And I'm going to have to negotiate some deal with him. Like, in complete sentences. This is like meeting the biggest rock star in the world, and then asking him if you can date his daughter.

So went Everett's inner monologue as he walked with General Sulla back toward the town gate, wondering the whole time what the offer was, why they would come in person to make it, and whether the RoME soldiers or his fellow Lords would be the first to murder him when this whole situation blew up in his face.

The town seemed to get further away with every step. The silence was beyond awkward. General Sulla kept pace with Lord Starr, but while the latter's gait was stiff and urgent, the former fairly glided along, chin level and eyes taking in the sights.

Finally accepting that somebody had to say *something*, Everett cleared his throat. "I've heard so much about you....Is it true—?"

"Probably not," General Sulla interrupted, still looking forward. "'The General never sleeps,'" he said with fake awe. "'Sulla can wield two bows at the same time!' 'General Sulla can come back after being executed!'"

Lord Starr's shoulders slumped a little. "Oh...I guess that means you don't have one of the six Slaked Swords..."

The Slaked Swords are the most powerful and coveted weapons in the game, created with the finest blades from each realm, and forged in the collected blood of each of the ten Dragon Guardians. They were crazy hard to make, and nobody can even craft them anymore because some kid tried duping them and ruined it for everyone else.

The General stopped walking and took a deep breath. "No, I don't have one of those," he replied. "I have two." When Lord Starr looked up to face him, Sulla pointed a thumb back at his scabbard. "The other one is back in our base. I never carry them at the same time."

Everett snuck a peek at the ornate sheath strapped across Sulla's back. The blade was a good five feet long and probably as wide as his thigh. The hilt, the crossguard, and the scabbard itself were all absolute works of art. His breath caught in his throat.

"You want to hold it?" General Sulla asked, scanning the horizon.

Lord Starr emitted a series of random sounds and moved in a way that pretty accurately simulated a mild stroke.

"You want to hold it. Here." Sulla unfastened the leather clasps around the crossguard. As he drew the blade free, a brilliant metallic ringing filled the air. The razor-sharp blade flashed in the sunlight, and Everett could see blood and fire swirling within the metal as if it were a living thing.

When Sulla laid the weapon in his hands, Everett bobbled it a moment but kept it aloft. Despite its outlandish size, the sword almost floated on his palms, so that he could easily take it by the grip and turn it in the air to further admire its flawless construction.

"Give it a swing," The General urged. "Just be careful where you point it." They were only about a hundred yards from the town walls now, and the other Lords were watching them from the open gate with, no doubt, deepening anxiety.

Everett put both hands on the hilt, gave the sword a few warm-up shakes to gauge the way it moved, and then performed his signature sword art, a whirling cross-slash with an upswing finisher. The sword moved through the air fluidly, and with his final stroke, balls of flame burst from the tip, soaring into the sky and exploding in hellish blue lightning.

"Good thing you didn't try a down-thrust." Sulla casually took the sword from Lord Starr's trembling hands and sheathed it. "Come along, now," he said, clapping Lord Starr on the shoulder, "let's not keep your fellow Lords waiting."

About ten minutes later, they entered the grand conference room in the town hall. The Lords were seated at the elliptical conference table, while General Sulla stood at the bank of large windows that faced the Square.

"General Sulla, it is of course a great honor to have you here in our humble town," Lord Baneblade said. "We have never had dealings with the RoME clan, nor have any of us knowingly crossed any of your clan members. I do hope that if any wrong has been done, we can reach an amicable solution."

The Lords waited in tense silence, watching Sulla's immobile back.

"A bloody crime," The General muttered after a lengthy silence. "What the Bleak Clan does...there's no sense to it. No courage. No honor." He turned to face the assembled Lords, arms clasped behind him, his visage grim.

"What most of us earn through hard work, through great sacrifice, through a genuine respect for the realms, they seek to steal, to destroy, to kill." The

General seemed lost in thought for a moment after he said this, his fingers tracing a scar that ran from behind his ear down his neck and toward his right shoulder.

Lord Forlani leaned forward now, putting an elbow on the table. "Lord Starr informed us that you wished to make an offer. As you can see, we don't have much of value compared to a clan of your standing, especially after our recent run-in with the Bleak Clan—"

General Sulla whirled toward the table, driving his fists into the tabletop. "Exactly! Your recent run-in with Bleak Clan was *because* of how very much you have of value. Your recent success at the Shattered Peak Dungeons is no secret—word has reached all seven realms, and the target on your back is as big as the sky."

He straightened, holding his arms wide. "Every time a clan acquires items of great power or value, Jake da Rippa and his horde of bandits raids them, running off with the loot, desolating the buildings, and executing players for no other reason than their own sick amusement."

Lord Celt shifted in his seat, twisting his russet beard. He finally spoke up: "So what can we do about it? What offer do you propose, General Sulla?"

As The General looked toward the North, toward the Restless Sea, his face took on an awful aspect. "I offer this: revenge on Jake and the entire Bleak Clan, and an end to all the unrest they sow."

CHAPTER 13
THE PLAN

"Yeah, I know it won't be *easy*, but it's doable." Everett sat on his living room couch with his phone on one knee, slouched over a math packet.

"Says the guy who doesn't have a blood marker on his head," Alex replied from the screen on Everett's phone. Everett wanted to invite him over to hash the invasion plan out, but he didn't want to break his mom's rules. At least, not any more of her rules.

Everett's mom sat at her desk in the corner, neglecting her reheated dinner and tapping away on her laptop ever since she got home an hour ago. That was only about two minutes after Everett managed to pack the Interface gear back in its original box and hide it back in her closet.

Alex twirled a pencil next to his ear. "So is Sulla as awesome as everyone says he is?"

"Um, awesomer. Very intense, but super cool. He

let me wield one of his Slaked Swords."

"Shut up! Do you have any idea—those things are like impossible to even *look at*! And you got to see it through the Interface—I mean, how cool is—" Everett suddenly had a coughing fit. His mom looked over from her corner quizzically. He pantomimed something between a wasp attacking him and a fire in the kitchen before hurrying for the steps.

"Dude!" Everett whisper-shouted as he closed his bedroom door. "My mom didn't give me the Interface yet. I was on a sneak preview."

"Wait—Everett Starner broke a *rule*?" Alex adopted a raspy voice. "You are one of usssss now!"

Everett chuckled and sat on his bed. "So, what do you think of the plan? Do you think we have a shot?"

Everett could hear Alex slumping back in his creaky leather gaming chair; he was getting serious. "We have RoME clan on our side. How could we lose? I just wonder why they even want our help. I mean, they can crush anyone they want, right?"

Everett set his phone down and started unwinding his VR equipment. It sucked to go back to the old setup, but the thrill of the plan was enough to offset the disappointment. "I really think Sulla meant it when he said he wanted to help us out. He said he's sick of Jake terrorizing everyone that gets a little bit of power."

"And maybe Sulla wanted a look at some of the

loot from the Conference of Mages," Alex suggested, an obvious edge to his voice. "I mean, you saw what Zero used to drive the Bleakers out of town—we have some top-tier spells, and I'm sure the Lords are hiding certain unique items we haven't even seen. There's gotta be something in it for RoME clan."

"Maybe," Everett said, trying not to sound offended. "But if we have a powerful ally on our side, and the Bleakers out of commission, I think sharing some loot is worth it."

"As long as that powerful ally *stays* on our side," Alex said darkly.

Everett plugged in his headset and adjusted the settings. "Yeah, well, that's a risk I'm willing to take. And if it doesn't work out, I mean, it's just a game, right?"

Alex guffawed. "Riiiight. And Kit is *just* another clan member."

"Don't even bring her up—"

"I just hope she really is a *her*, and not some forty-year-old dude creepin' on you."

"Whatever," Everett said, laughing.

"You gonna hop on party chat so we can all get this plan figured out?"

"Yeah, but only for a few minutes. I have to be up early tomorrow for church."

A few minutes later, Everett was plugged back in, conferencing with some of the leaders of RoME and

Lordz about his strategy for the strike against Bleak Clan. The RoME leaders seemed genuinely impressed with the plan, and Lord Baneblade said he'd be happy to spread the word to the rest of the Lords.

General Sulla made it very clear he was in charge of this entire coalition effort. He had a way of determining what the Bleak Clan members were up to, including when Jake was logged in—he wouldn't share many details, and nobody was eager to press him on it. Since players can't be harmed when they're logged out, that was obviously crucial information for this attack.

They'd be on watch in shifts since they're spread out across time zones, so whoever was on alert when Bleak was vulnerable would get the call, so to speak. Everett desperately wanted to get that call. He put a few hours in, drilling some clan members on the plan of attack, but it seemed like Jake was done for the day, so Everett decided to call it a night.

He went to bed but was so excited he couldn't fall asleep right away. When he finally drifted off, he dreamed of buildings and statues, of Bleakers and The General. But mostly he dreamed of Kit.

CHAPTER 14
SICK

Everett groaned and scrunched up his face, burrowing into his pillow. His mom pulled back the covers, expecting some resistance but finding none.

"Ev, honey? What's wrong?"

"My head...it's killing me." He tried squinting at her, but the daylight beaming through his blinds drove him back undercover.

She checked her phone and then scratched her forehead with her thumb. "Were you up late last night? When I checked on you at 9:00, you said you were getting off that game—"

"I did, I was off by 10:00. I don't know—it just hit me."

"Do you think eating something would help? I made pancakes..."

"No, I'm not—" He gagged.

She leaned forward and rubbed his back. "I'll stay

home with you, all right? I just need to find someone to cover for me on worship team."

Everett forced himself to sit up. "No, no, I'm—I don't need you to stay home. I'm just going to lay in bed." He made the herculean effort of opening his eyes. "Seriously, Mom, you can go. I'll be fine."

His mom checked her phone again and stood up. "Well, you need something in your stomach so you can take medicine. Can you make it downstairs, or do I need to bring something up?"

He flopped back and draped an arm over his face. "I'll be down in five minutes. Can I just have a plain pancake and some juice?"

She confirmed his order and hastened downstairs. By the time Everett shambled down the steps, his breakfast was ready, his mother standing anxiously beside it. "Are you sure you're OK by yourself? I still feel bad leaving you home alone all day yesterday—"

Everett shuffled over to her, brows heavy. "It's just church and then back home, right? I'll be asleep the whole time anyway." He hiked up one corner of his mouth. "If I'm better, maybe I can help with your garden?"

His mom got a little misty-eyed. "Oh, Everett Lee...you are the sweetest boy." She gave him a gentle but emphatic hug. "Oh, and I have something for you when I get back. It's a surprise."

He took a bite of dry pancake and forced it down. "Just for helping in the garden? I didn't even do anything yet."

She slipped into her shoes as she slung her purse over her shoulder. "No, I got for you before. I wanted to give it to you yesterday but—" She waved off her own comment. "Anyway, maybe this afternoon, if you're feeling better."

Everett raised his eyebrows. "I'm feeling better just thinking what it might be..."

"Just wait until you see it, then tell me that," she said, truly smiling for the first time.

"If you insist," Everett joked.

She made for the door. "All right, take care. Drink plenty of fluids and get your rest."

"I will," Everett said, popping some Advil as a farewell and chasing it down with some OJ.

In another minute, he had polished off the rest of his breakfast and marched upstairs. Instead of turning left at the top of the steps to go to his room, he went right. He entered his mom's room and made for her closet. He found the box right where he left it.

As he hustled to his room to play with the Interface one last time—at least, until his mom officially gave it to him—the only thing he forgot was the rest of the juice he was supposed to finish. That, and his anti-seizure pill on the counter right beside it.

CHAPTER 15
THE INVASION

When Lord Starr logged on and appeared in his new manor on the Square, he checked his messages. Not seeing much news, he DMed General Sulla for an update.

The General responded almost instantly: Rippa has not logged in since yesterday, so the Bleak Clan is still laying low. Sulla assured him that he would let everyone know when Jake's active.

Wanting to make the most of the hour or so he had until his mom got home, Everett decided to double-check his team and make sure they have their part of the invasion down pat.

Kit, Wolfgang, and Miracle were on Lord Starr's crew, along with a few newer guys who showed some promise on previous stealth missions. The main attack would hit the Bleak Clan's front gates full force, but Lord Starr was in charge of getting around to the back of the Bleaker's island undetected, and either breaching their weak side or at least distracting some of the defenders from guarding the front. It wasn't the most glamorous part of the invasion, but Everett was honestly thrilled to be involved at all. Who knows, maybe they'd make all the difference.

"All right," Lord Starr said to the group, "our priority is to draw as little attention as possible while being ready to pack a punch once they notice us. Does everyone have their optimal gear sets on?"

The low-levs showed off their complete sets (several grades above anything they would dream of having at this stage, but middling by the "new normal" standards). Kit showed off her active stealth camo and throwing blades that returned directly to her hands. Miracle's armor was lightweight yet nearly impenetrable, and his prestiged bow was devastating.

"Do you even need the rest of us? Miracle has the whole mission on lock!" Wolfgang joked, earning laughs from all.

"That reminds me," Lord Starr said, checking his inventory. "I wanted to give you this." He held forth the Gungnir spear that Baneblade had gifted him when he became a Lord.

Wolfgang was speechless. He took the glowing spear with disbelief, examining its every inch. "Wow," he whispered. "Are you sure?"

"Yeah, of course." Lord Starr lightly shook Wolfgang's shoulder. "I'm more of a sword guy. You'll do more good with that thing than I ever would."

Wolfgang spent the next several minutes whirling Gungnir around and discharging random bursts of lightning here and there while the rest of the team discussed strategy. At the signal from Sulla, they would get in a clipper ship waiting off the northeast coast down from their town. They would circle wide to the east and approach Bleak Island from their least obvious side—much like the Bleakers had done during their raid on Lordz Landing.

Everett was laughing with Kit and Miracle at Wolfgang's fusion of ballet and violence when a message hit his ear: "The Snake Crawls."

Lord Starr's smile faded, and his eyebrows drew together. "It's go time."

In no time, the whole group raced across town, through the eastern gate, and down to the natural harbor along the coast. Lord Starr took the helm, and with a few tugs on the ropes, they were full sail toward Bleak Island.

The sunset gilded the ocean to their right, where Lord Starr could see the silhouettes of dozens of RoME triremes cutting effortlessly through the sea. The cliffs of Lordz Landing shrank behind them, and soon Lord Starr's crew was surrounded by boundless water on all sides.

"So," Wolfgang said, "is this the first time on a cruise for anyone else?"

The noobs raised their hands, and Wolfgang nodded, leaning on his spear in an attempt to look cool. The obvious nausea on his face neutralized that effort.

"I like to stand near the front of the ship, and just watch the horizon," Kit said. "We should be there in about twenty minutes."

"Yeah, I can be lookout," Wolfgang offered, grateful for the advice.

Kit stood by Lord Starr and consulted the world map. "You'll want to veer right about five degrees. We need to stay out of sight until we draw parallel with the island."

Lord Starr turned the wheel slightly, and they could see the RoME ships shrinking away to the west. "Can we pick up any more speed?" he asked. "I want to get there ahead of the main fleet as much as possible."

Kit nodded and teamed up with Miracle to adjust the riggings toward the prevailing winds. The noobs gravitated to the bow with Wolfgang, who had lost his greenish complexion.

With the sea air in his face, Lord Starr swelled with confidence about this mission. These Bleakers will finally get a taste of their own medicine. Even if they don't do a ton of damage, it'll feel good just to make a strike. And with RoME on their side, what's the worst that could happen?

As the sun dipped into the sea, their ship gained a few knots and Lord Starr gripped the wheel tighter to keep from pitching backward. "ETA, Kit?" he called out.

She hustled back to the quarterdeck. "About six minutes out now. We'll be on level with Bleak Island any moment here, so you can start drawing left to swing around toward our landing point."

Lord Starr spun the wheel, sending the ship in a broad arc toward the sunset. He couldn't speak for the others, but Lord Starr felt his heart begin to pound as the speck on the horizon grew to a rock, and from a rock to a crenelated fortress on a steep and craggy island. Giant torches burned at the top of the ten towers ringing the Bleak stronghold, creating an almost hypnotic sight.

"I'm starting to feel sick, too," Kit said, "and it has nothing to do with the waves."

Lord Starr completely empathized but put on a brave face. "We're not storming the place, just causing a little disruption. We might not even have to leave the boat."

"I don't know if that's reassuring or not," Wolfgang groaned, leaning over the side.

The Bleak fortress loomed ever closer. Lord Starr feathered the rudder, drawing off speed. He then gave the order to back the mainsail and throw out the anchor, bringing them to a halt just shy of the shallows.

MiracleMan climbed the riggings to scope out the ramparts. "There are barely any guards on this side," he said. "And soon, there will be none at all." He balanced on the highest spar and unslung his bow.

Aiming every which way but toward the fortress, Miracle fired off ten arrows in as many seconds. The crew looked toward the ramparts, confused.

"Um, Miracle?" Wolfgang said. "Were you trying to see what it feels like to miss a shot for once?"

"Hang on," he replied, his eyes fixed on the walls.

Moments later, the crew observed dark forms plummeting from the top of the fortress and onto the rocks below.

"How the—?" Kit stammered.

Miracle slid down to the deck. "Reflex arrows. I can shoot them out and they angle back at the target from a different direction. Keeps the enemy from figuring out which way the shots came from."

While everyone else admired the brilliance of that tactic, Wolfgang frowned. "Yeah, but you don't want to do *too* good of a job going unnoticed. We are the distraction, right?"

Just then, they heard a commotion from the eastern ramparts.

"Happy now?" Kit asked. "They noticed."

Lord Starr furrowed his brow at the noise swelling on the dark ramparts. "I hate to say it, but we'd probably be safer getting off. We need to find cover on the island before they spot the boat."

Everyone clambered off the ship, slogged through the knee-high surf, and scuffled up onto a narrow spit.

Meanwhile, the commotion above grew louder. When Lord Starr looked up, he saw the fire on the closest tower divide into a dozen smaller flames. A shout reached his ear just as the fires arced and grew—flaming arrows flying in their direction. They all flew long of the crew, but three hit the ship. The deck and sails bloomed red and orange in seconds.

"Good news, Wolfgang," Kit said, watching the boat burn. "You won't be getting seasick anymore."

CHAPTER 16
THE BIG FREEZE

Lord Starr's invasion force picked their way along the shore, their ears straining for any sign of further Bleaker attacks. So far, they heard only the crash of waves against the rocks and the wind through the few scattered trees.

Lets cut up that way, Lord Starr suggested through a group text. The team trudged uphill and soon reached the foot of what looked like a cliff, but was actually home to a concealed footpath that hugged the cliffside up to, hopefully, an entrance.

With Wolfgang on point and Kit bringing up the rear, the procession climbed slowly up hundreds of feet. One of the noobs lost his footing and Lord Starr caught him by the arm just in time. He held him dangling in the air for a heart-stopping moment before swinging him back to the ledge.

Thx, sir! the freckle-faced soldier messaged.

No prob, Lord Starr replied. *No need 4 sir tho ...u*

can just call me "Lord".

The noob's eyes widened, so Lord Starr flashed him a smile and patted him on the back, which almost sent the guy off the edge again.

They eventually reached a level spot with just enough room to fit the seven of them. It was so dark now that everyone was basically groping along the cliff face for any sign of a way forward.

Wolf, Lord Starr DMed. *U want to get noticed, rite? Lite it up w/ ur spear and c if we get any fans.*

Wolfgang laughed out loud, causing a resounding echo. Everyone exchanged surprised looks.

"Guys, over here!" Kit rasped, giving up on the silent communication. "A passageway! I think it goes up to the top of the walls."

The group hustled into the cave-like opening and found a stairway that spiraled up into darkness. Voices carried down from somewhere above, which was confirmation enough to Lord Starr to wave everybody on.

Five breathless minutes later—it was amazing how exhausting just *imagining* you were running up steps could be—they reached a hatch in the ceiling.

Lord Starr put his hand on the handle and leaned down to face the rest of his team. "All right, guys, on the count of three, I'll pop this hatch. Be ready for anything, OK?"

His companions gripped their weapons and

nodded intensely. "Here we go. One...two...THREE!"

The hatch flung open, and the group burst out of the opening onto the fortress' ramparts.

"AAAAAAAAAGGGHHHHHH!" they screamed, landing almost exactly in a circle formation, facing outward at...nothing?

Wolfgang, still screaming, let his voice trail off. He opened his eyes and cleared his throat. "Um, where is everyone? Miracle, did you kill the entire clan?"

"I'm good, but I'm not that good," Miracle quipped. His eyes scanned the walls all around. "No one is up here. Which means they're probably all—"

A thunderous crash from the south nearly shook them off their feet. As one, they whirled to look toward the sound. Ten stories below, inside the sprawling courtyard, a solid five-hundred Bleakers were massed in a broad crescent facing the main gate. At least, it used to be the main gate, before the RoME and Lordz clan forces erupted through with hellish fury.

"So, about our distraction..." Kit muttered.

The coalition forces continued to pour through the smashed gate, and they melted almost as quickly away under the relentless magic, missile fire, and general onslaught of the Bleakers.

"I kinda don't want their attention on us, ya know?" Wolfgang said.

"Hey, if they're not going to pay us any mind,"

Lord Starr said, "let's have fun being invisible."

Lord Starr had the group split into two—Miracle, Kit, and two of the low-levs were to go to the north end of the Bleak fortress and take out anyone they could find, while Wolfgang and the freckled noob would stick with Lord Starr on a raid-and-raze mission.

"If you get into any trouble," Lord Starr said to Kit, "make for the RoME ships. I'm sure they have troops hanging back to extract everyone once this ends." She gave him a warm smile, her purple eyes gleaming in the moonlight. Then, she turned and led her squad off toward the stairway for the north side.

Lord Starr looked at the noob and Wolfgang. "Who wants to grief some Bleakers?"

The noob cracked his knuckles and smiled. Wolfgang slammed the butt of his spear into the ground, sending a huge bolt of lightning into the sky.

"C'mon," Lord Starr said, turning toward the stairs down to the east end, "before you get so excited you kill us all."

In minutes, they were at ground level, skulking along the wall to avoid the ever-growing free-for-all in the center of town. They searched the first few buildings they came across and found very little of interest. Then they saw the armory, with only two guards out front.

"That place is huge!" the noob raved, then clapped

his hands over his mouth. "They gotta have some primo stuff in there," he whispered.

"I'll take care of those clowns," Wolfgang assured them, swaggering forward with a twirl of his spear. He reached the corner of the building opposite the armory and poised his spear. With a primal howl, Wolfgang raised his spear, an electric blue flare lighting up the sky. He leaped forward and thrust Gungnir toward the hapless guards.

Except he didn't reach the guards. In mid-flight, Wolfgang froze, poised to strike but never striking.

It seemed like time stopped. Lord Starr and the noob stared out from the shadows, unable to breathe.

The guards, startled, jumped back. Then they noticed Wolfgang wasn't moving. They regained their courage. First one, then the other, crept over, spears at the ready. They exchanged looks. With a nod, they struck. They mercilessly skewered Wolfgang over and over again. Lord Starr and the noob did nothing but watch in shock.

Wolfgang's body collapsed to the ground, his spear rolling from his lifeless hand. One of the guards bent down to claim his spoils. In a flash, Lord Starr closed the distance between himself and the guards, freeing his Crystal Triblade on the way. Before either guard could react, he unleashed a fatal combo that relieved them of their heads.

Retrieving Gungnir from the growing pool of

Wolfgang's blood, Lord Starr stared at his friend's fallen body for a long time. He had certainly seen his friend fall in combat before, but something seemed off. His body wasn't fading away so that it could respawn back in Lordz Landing.

"Wolfgang," Lord Starr called to his friend. "Alex? Are you AFK?"

Everett got no response. In fact, he felt like the whole world was muted.

The noob trotted over and hesitantly nudged him. Lord Starr shook his head back into the present. It wasn't just in his head—the whole town was quieter. To be sure, there was still the chaos of hundreds of people fighting all around, but it sounded different now. Calmer, somehow, but in an eerie way.

"What the heck?" the noob uttered in disbelief. "What should we do?"

"Fight, or die," Lord Starr said through gritted teeth.

Throwing caution to the wind, Lord Starr and the noob headed toward the action. They wove down a few alleyways before emerging in the expansive courtyard, some thousand yards across. What they both saw astonished them.

Scattered about, scores of players—Bleakers, RoMANS, and Lordz—stood like statues, and the still living raced around slaughtering or defending them. Magic blazed across the open space in all directions, and arrows hailed down, but everyone seemed oblivious of anything beyond their pocket of action.

In the midst of it all, General Sulla raged about, mowing through Bleakers without a break in stride. He was screaming for Jake to show his face, oblivious to the damage raining down on him. All around, buildings burned, raiders ran off with loot, and NPCs were captured. The Bleak Clan was being devastated, but something felt horribly wrong.

Lord Starr laid into a crowd of Bleakers surrounding a pair of frozen RoMANS, leveling them all and executing the last one. His fury knew no bounds. This was far from his first battle, but every time a body shuddered under his sword, his stomach revolted. He managed to shoulder up to a band of fellow clan members close to the main gate, and they staved off a disorderly charge of Bleakers while slowly withdrawing.

From the swirling storm of blades and ash and gore, General Sulla charged toward them, enraged. "The coward has fled! Back to the boats!" He barreled toward the gaping main gate, and it was all Lord Starr and his brothers-in-arms could do to stay on the furious leader's heels.

Bounding onto a trireme, Lord Starr looked back at the collapsing Bleak fortress. He remembered Kit and Miracle were still in there, but his ship began pulling away as he messaged them to make a run for it.

As the smoldering island receded in the distance, he ached to hear his friends' voices but heard nothing except the Restless Sea.

CHAPTER 17
HEAVY

Dawn painted the sky a faded purple as players straggled back into Lordz Landing in twos and threes. As they trudged up the hill from the shore, they seemed defeated, even though they were returning as nominal victors. It had only been a couple of hours in real life, but Lord Starr dragged as if he had been awake for days.

At the sight of the ramparts, many picked up the pace, eager to reunite with their fallen friends when they respawned in town. The lookouts on the wall called down greetings and ordered the eastern gate to be opened for them.

As soon as the first warriors reached the gate, the RoMANS who stayed behind almost pounced on them.

A gladiator reached them first. "You wouldn't believe what happened while you were gone!"

A centurion was next. "How did you guys raid Bleak without taking any casualties?"

"Did you lose contact with everyone else, too?" a legionary asked.

Lord Starr and his new best friend, The Freckled Noob, exchanged looks, then followed the crowd into town.

As the Square filled with the returning fighters, those who stayed back gathered around them. Lord Forlani had stayed behind with the RoMAN contingent, so he took Lord Starr aside to discuss matters. They walked together down the main street leading to the west end. With everyone else gathered in the Square, they were able to talk normally without anyone eavesdropping.

"We did not expect you back already," Lord Forlani said. "We've been waiting for the fallen to return to the inn, but none ever came. We assumed you hadn't reached Bleak Island yet."

Lord Starr stiffened. "Oh, we made it there all right. And as you saw, not all of us came back. People on all sides suddenly froze, and when they were killed, their bodies didn't fade out..." His voice caught in his throat.

Forlani placed a hand on Lord Starr's shoulder and furrowed his brow. "I assume you were unable to communicate with anyone else unless you were standing with them like we are now?"

Lord Starr nodded.

"Then I guess the big question now," Lord Forlani said, "is what do we do about this?" He gestured toward the Shieldbreaker monument, where eight clan members stood around in various poses, as still as the statue in the center.

As Lord Starr looked at the surreal scene, his stomach sank. What was going on? It all happened so fast—Wolfgang rushed those guards, the sky flashed blue, and then he froze. When he died, he didn't disappear, he just dropped...

The spear. Lord Starr took out Gungnir and looked it over, handling it like a sleeping cobra. Did this cause everything?

Lord Forlani waved a hand in front of Starr's face to break his trance. "Come along—we must return to the Square. Perhaps we can get to the bottom of this if we all put our heads together."

When Everett turned to head back to the Square with Lord Forlani, it was like he was moving underwater. His arms were weights at his side. A low, sustained tone throbbed in his head, like a jet engine winding down. The buildings all around were the same—the houses, the inn, the smithy, all of it—but it was like he was visiting some other place entirely.

They stepped into the Square, and a large crowd filled the area. Lord Forlani climbed atop a flat wagon that served as a stage, and Lord Starr followed him.

The murmurings of the crowd died down, and Forlani invited Lord Starr to speak.

Lord Starr looked toward the south gate as a few more players filtered in. Deciding to get this over with, he cleared his throat. "The attack on the Bleak Clan was a success," he announced. "We got them back for the havoc they caused here. We destroyed a lot of their buildings, raided their warehouses—"

"Yeah, and lost a bunch of people in the process!" a grim-faced Valkyrie shouted from the middle of the crowd. "Who cares about loot? We want our friends back!"

The crowd began to grumble, getting louder. "We want lives, not more loot!" they chanted.

"We're not sure why the fallen have not respawned yet, but we're hoping it's just a lag issue," Lord Starr shouted, holding his hands out toward the assembly. "Plus, we're still waiting for the last of the ships to return."

"I was on the last ship." Everyone turned to look at a tall, dark-skinned warrior toward the back. "We're all here. No one else is coming back."

A silence fell over the Square. Lord Starr's heart thundered in his chest. His helmet grew hot, and sweat beaded on his forehead and neck.

"We'll have more answers once we all have a chance to discuss what we've seen," he faltered. "I'm sure there's an explanation for everything."

Any sense of decorum left the crowd as a hundred questions and complaints spewed forth.

"Why did people freeze?"

"Why did we get affected here if the battle was across the sea?"

"Where are all the NPCs?"

"Is this some kind of curse?"

"Who made this guy a Lord?"

"I'll tell you what he can do with all that stupid loot—"

Everett couldn't take this anymore. He had to call Kit. He had to go over to Alex's house and see what happened. He had to log out of the game.

Except he couldn't.

CHAPTER 18
HOMECOMING

Lord Starr's stomach swirled. The sun beat down twice as hot. His sword weighed a ton. *What is going on?*

"Forlani...can you log out?"

Lord Forlani fidgeted a moment, then stared. "No." He stepped forward to address the crowd. "Everyone, please...can anyone here log out? Maybe we can figure out what's wrong from the outside."

The crowd quieted, people shifting and then becoming still. Nervous murmuring swelled to mild panic. Lord Forlani raised his hands to quell the rising tide. "So everyone that's still here is on the Interface?" He pulled his chin. "There's—there has to be a reasonable explanation for this. It's probably just a hardware issue..."

Lord Starr placed a hand on Forlani's shoulder and lowered his voice. "I'm new to this Interface thing. Does it normally feel this...heavy?"

Forlani shook his head. A distant clamor drew his eyes, as well as the crowd's, to the south.

"Miracle? Miracle?!" Kit came racing into the Square, but skidded to a halt when she saw the crowd. "Where's MiracleMan?"

Lord Starr hopped down from the wagon and circled around to her. She met him halfway, by the inn. "Kit, what happened? How did you get back?"

She took him aside, aware of prying ears. When she finally looked at him again, her eyes sent dread into his heart. "We were on the north side of the Bleaker town, picking off stragglers. The noobs went down pretty quick, but Miracle and I avoided detection for a long time.

"We found the manors of the Bleak leaders, and I snooped around while Miracle played lookout. There were some great items I jacked, but nobody was lurking around. We figured everyone was part of the action at the gate."

They had walked a block from the Square, but she double-checked that no one was spying on them before she continued. "Then we heard someone yelling—like a battle cry, coming toward us. We saw a Bleaker run out between two burning buildings and dash down an alleyway. Right on his tail was Sulla, still yelling. He disappeared down the alley after the Bleaker and then—well, the weirdest thing happened..."

Lord Starr clenched his jaw. "Let me guess: a flash of blue light."

Kit's eyes went wide. "You saw it, too?" Lord Starr nodded. "A minute later Sulla charged out of the alley and took off in another direction, still raging. I turned to Miracle to have him follow me, but he was...frozen."

Lord Starr put his hands on his hips and shook his head at the ground. "The same thing happened to Wolfgang. That flash of light, he froze and then..." He couldn't bring himself to say the rest.

Kit put a hand on his arm and searched his eyes. "We will figure out what happened to him...to everyone. This isn't—this is just a game, right?"

"Yeah," he said, sounding like he wasn't even convinced himself.

They marched back to the Square. Lord Forlani stood with Lord Celt by the Town Hall, looking like they were competing for the most freaked-out expression. Lord Starr all but dragged Kit over to the two, who looked up and restored their Lordly miens in the presence of a lady.

Kit nudged Lord Starr, who took a deep breath. "Has anyone been talking about a blue flash of light?"

The Lords exchanged looks. Forlani tilted up his chin. Celt pursed his lips and then faced Kit and Starr. "We heard...grumblings about a light or a flash of something, right before a bunch of our guys—I don't know, lagged out? Froze?"

"It wasn't just ours," Lord Starr said. "RoME and Bleak also had guys freeze randomly. I saw some frozen guys get attacked, and when they went down...they stayed there." He felt like his breakfast was very eager to visit the cobblestones all of a sudden.

Lord Celt let this soak in a moment, his hand stroking his beard. He looked from Forlani to Starr to Kit, then shook his head. "I'm gonna get to the bottom of this..."

Celt started walking toward the wagon stage, but Lord Forlani caught him by the arm. "Celt...perhaps we should plan our next statement. We don't need to fan the flames anymore right now. If we start speculating about glitches or conspiracies or magic or whatever, we'll have a riot on our hands."

As if on cue, several clan members wandered over to the small gathering, led by ØGravityØ. Zero always looked intimidating, but having a small gang of stern-faced followers upped the effect dramatically. Even Forlani gulped when the mage stopped and hovered a few feet away.

Zero's hood tilted up, green eyes glowing from the shadowy recesses. "This is no magic. This curse runs deeper."

CHAPTER 19
BEHIND CLOSED DOORS

The jaws of Kit and the three Lords dropped simultaneously. The rest of the town continued their gossip, but it seemed like the sound had been sucked out of their particular corner of the Square.

Lord Celt regained the power of speech first. "You can talk?"

Lord Starr shook off his astonishment. "You're a girl?"

Zero looked up, pulled back her hood, and huffed. "Yeah, is that a problem?" The Lords shook their heads emphatically.

Zero threw up her hands. "What, do you think we all look like our characters? Was Shieldbreaker really a giant Viking? Does Lord Celt actually have bear claw scars on his face? You really think Kit has purple eyes?"

"Actually, I do. I have this rare condition called

'Alexandria's Genesis', which causes—"

"Not the time," Zero interrupted. "The point is, who I really am shouldn't matter here. And right now, who we are in the game seems to be who we are, period."

She looked to her sides at the small mob behind her. "We have a theory about what happened, but we don't want to cause more panic, or spoil any burgeoning alliances unduly."

Lords Forlani and Celt nodded solemnly, but Lord Starr's eyes shifted. Kit put her lips close to his ear. "She meant she doesn't want to tick off the RoME clan." He nodded like he knew that all along.

Celt looked to Forlani and then to Zero. "Perhaps we should go inside the hall here and discuss your theory." He eyed the crowd behind Zero. "To minimize concern, it would be best if just you came in with us." He placed a smile on top of his suggestion to sweeten it.

Zero gave her followers a long look and a nod. When she turned back, she pulled up her hood and glided toward the door. Forlani reached for the handle, but Zero flicked a wrist and the door swung open for her to hover right through.

Once the three Lords and Kit followed Zero into the Town Hall, Lord Forlani closed the door and hastened into the meeting hall to join them. The Lords took their customary places, while Kit stood by

Lord Starr, and Zero hovered in a dark corner by some bookshelves. No one mentioned it, but the emptiness of Lord Baneblade's chair tied a knot in everyone's heart.

Lord Celt drummed his fingers on the tabletop. "So what do you think happened, Zero?"

Zero drifted over to Lord Baneblade's spot at the head of the table and paused. "Whatever happened was not magic, and it might not have even been deliberate. Magic is either targeted or affects everyone—this event was random. Anyone who wanted to do harm to us wouldn't want to hurt their own people as well, even if they were trying to create plausible deniability."

Kit leaned close to Lord Starr, but he held up a hand. "I think I know what that one means," he whispered. "Like, if someone wants to look innocent, they try to cover their tracks." The squeeze of Kit's hand on his arm sent heat up his neck.

Lord Forlani rubbed his eye with his palm, then planted his hands on the table. "Could it be related to the Interface?"

Zero shrugged. "I don't know everyone who froze, but some of the ones I knew used VR, some used Interface. It does seem like only Interface users are here now, so..."

A distant pounding sound came from the front door. Celt looked to Lord Starr, then nodded toward the sound. Lord Starr saluted, which was awkwardly formal, then hustled out.

When he opened the door, he faced the most absurd sight yet, which was really saying something. A chubby little dwarf with big anime eyes stared up at him. The dwarf had a sparkly red unitard and tutu on. In his fat hand he held a monstrous battleaxe, the shaft longer than the dwarf was tall, and the head broader than his plump torso. His gamertag hovered over his head.

"CuddlyMooMoo?" Lord Starr couldn't reconcile the cartoonish figure before him with the dead-serious expression on his round face. "Um, sorry, but this is a closed session. The Lords will address the public shortly." He winced at that last word, but it didn't seem to offend the dwarf.

"Everstarr, is that you?" The voice sounded familiar. Commanding. Scandinavian?

"Shieldbreaker?" The dwarf seemed aware of his appearance for the first time and shifted uncomfortably. He looked away and nodded. "But why—I mean, you look..."

The dwarf gripped his axe and shook it angrily. "When that Bleaker scum executed me, I couldn't use my old account anymore. I had to convince my kid sister to let me start over on hers. The deal was...I had to let her pick my gamertag and avatar." He pinched the edges of his tutu and muscled his way through a curtsey. "CuddlyMooMoo, requesting membership to the Lordz Clan."

Lord Starr suppressed a laugh. The crowd was still mostly clustered in the Square, intent on their own discussions, but several people started craning their necks toward the Town Hall. "C'mon," he said, waving CuddlyMooMoo inside.

Once the door was closed, Lord Starr returned to his normal tone and volume. He didn't mean to, but when he addressed CuddlyMooMoo, he put his hands on his knees and bent forward a little. "So, we're trying to figure out what's going on with all the weirdness lately—"

CuddlyMooMoo arched a brow. "Seriously? I'm not a toddler. For cryin' out loud..." He climbed onto a chair in the hallway and looked Lord Starr in the eye. "Better?"

Lord Starr blushed and nodded. "Sorry. Anyway, you must have heard about people disappearing, and how no one can log out—"

"Yeah, I noticed that when I logged in. How long has it been like this?"

"Wait, you just got here?" The dwarf nodded. "How long ago?"

He shrugged. "Maybe twenty minutes ago? I got this account set up and spawned outside of town. There was almost nobody here, so I ran to my secret hiding spot and snagged this bad boy without anyone noticing me. Great statue on the west end, by the way." He winked.

"Then I saw you guys coming back in boats, and I overheard a bunch of stuff I couldn't make sense of. Like what's this about people disappearing? Did Jake clip more of our guys?"

Lord Starr pressed his lips together. "Maybe you should come with me."

They entered the meeting room, everyone speechless as the sparkly dwarf waddled over to Shieldbreaker's old spot and climbed atop the seat. He cleared his throat and spread out his arms. "Brother Lords, Zero, cute cat girl...I am back."

Lord Starr ventured a smile when the eyes in the room shifted from the pudgy, sequined dwarf to him. His arms tried to start talking, but his mouth didn't contribute anything intelligible.

"Why is everyone so..." CuddlyMooMoo unslung the axe from his back and slammed it into the table, nearly halving it. Everyone jumped back—even Zero, which was a sight in itself.

"Shieldbreaker?" A grin crept across Zero's face. "You crazy—awesome disguise, dude!"

The dwarf scratched the back of his neck. "Disguise...yeah." He rubbed his hands together. "So, catch me up. What's happened since I, ya know, left?"

Everyone began talking at once, and the dwarf's head swiveled back and forth. He held up his meaty hands, but they kept going.

Suddenly, the front door burst open, and everyone stopped. Footsteps thundered into the meeting room.

Four RoMANs, their faces tight with panic and exertion, staggered to a stop. Slung between them was the massive form of Sulla. His grim head, the only part of him not covered in steel, hung upside-down, listless.

One of the wild-eyed soldiers stared at the Lords. "Poisoned! The General's been poisoned!"

CHAPTER 20
VISITORS

Lord Celt rushed over to the RoMANs and helped heft The General onto the table. Forlani stepped alongside them, worry creasing his brow. "What happened?"

The tallest of the four soldiers, a sour-faced man tagged CrassusVII, squared himself to Forlani. "We returned to RoME after the battle at the Bleak fortress. Our NPCs are gone. No one has respawned. We can't log out of the game. Sulla told us to ride here to see what fate you faced. When he approached your southern gate, The General fell from his horse." His expression wavered between despair and accusation. "Ever since, he's been like this."

Lord Celt caught the drift right away, however subtle it was meant to be. "We had nothing to do with this—with Sulla or anyone else dropping out or freezing or whatever is going on here!"

"Jake..."

Everyone turned toward the man sprawled on the table. The General's eyes slowly opened, his mouth working on more syllables.

"Jake...is behind this. He has infected us all..." Sulla tried to lift his head, but it thumped back down. Lord Starr offered a hand to help him sit up, but Sulla weakly waved it off. The General closed his eyes and took a deep breath, then heaved himself up to sitting.

Those gathered around took a step back to give Sulla room to swing his legs over the side of the table. After steadying himself on the edge, he tipped forward to his feet. His balance held.

With another deep breath, he drew himself up, regaining his awful dignity. The old fire in his eyes reignited as he looked at each person in the room. "So," he said, some gravel still in his voice. "We are faced with a grave danger."

The RoMANs and Lordz exchanged looks, each implying that the other group was the danger in question. The General looked past them all, toward the far side of the room. The others watched him as he marched over and gazed out of the windows facing the Square.

"Our people—RoMANs and Lordz—are scared and have no clue what happened. They will rise up in fear if we don't give them answers. We must get out there and tell them *something* to maintain order." He turned to face the room, clenching his jaw. "Then, we go after the Bleak Clan and finish them, once and for all."

Everyone struggled to breathe again, but when they did, they felt no lighter. Most of them looked down at the table, but Zero and the dwarf faced Sulla unfazed.

"How do we know that won't make things worse?" CuddlyMooMoo unslung his axe and aimed it toward the north. "Isn't attacking the Bleak Clan what brought this on in the first place?"

The General seemed to notice the dwarf for the first time and masked his disdain and confusion well. "We're obviously the victims of some bizarre spell, or hack, or—frankly, I don't know. But we cannot let the Bleakers terrorize us any longer!"

Kit held her hands forth hesitantly and gritted a smile. "But they were frozen too. It doesn't seem like they would poison themselves if they were behind it."

Sulla dismissed her suggestion with a flip of his hand. "Maybe they didn't know what they were doing." He began pacing, a hand on his brow. "We have to decide what to tell the people so they're calm while we plan our assault. I can bring the full force of RoME down on them—"

Lord Forlani held up a hand to intercept Sulla as he walked by. "General, please...are you sure you're well enough to make any big plans right now?" He looked around for support, but no one chimed in. "Do we know the full extent of this...event? Has anyone contacted any other clans? Are we the only ones affected?"

Sulla threw up his arms. "We can't communicate with anyone unless it's face to face now. For all I know, we're the only clans left!"

Lord Celt walked over beside Sulla and Forlani, his head tilted slightly. "I agree we need to do something. And we need to give our people answers. But," he said, placing a hand on each man's shoulder, "I won't lie to my clan. And I won't send us into another battle without knowing what we're up against."

Sulla grunted and turned away, rubbing the scar on the back of his neck. "Fine. But tell them something soon...I won't have my men wait around here for your town to eat itself alive."

CuddlyMooMoo walked across the table to join the discussion. "And in the meantime, what? We're still people playing a game, right? I mean, I still have a body somewhere that needs to...do things. I drank a lot of Mountain Dew before I logged on this morning..."

Everyone began to shuffle uneasily. A few guys started bouncing in place.

Lord Celt looked around the room. "All right, let's go out there. But I'm telling my people that we're still looking for answers, not looking for trouble."

Lord Starr cleared his throat. "Maybe we should interview some people, see if their stories match up? We might find out some more clues about what exactly happened over there, and back here."

Lord Celt looked up and squinted one eye. "This is turning into Ye Olde CSI." He waved everyone along and trooped outside.

In the Square, dozens of people watched three Lords, The General, a mage, a cat-girl, and a bearded ball of glitter leave the Town Hall and proceed toward the wagon stage. The Lords ascended the wagon, with Lord Celt up front. He commanded their attention without a word and spoke once the crowd was silent.

"Fellow clan members, we want to give you some answers about the recent problems we've encountered. We want to...but we can't. All we know now is that RoME clan is experiencing similar troubles, and magic does not seem to be involved." He looked toward Sulla and Zero, down at ground level. The mage nodded solemnly, and Sulla merely clenched his jaw.

"We know you're scared—truth be told, so are we—but we have to remain calm. Blaming people without the facts will lead to anarchy. Whoever did this is probably hoping we do just that. Don't give them the satisfaction. We are a clan. As long as we stick together, we'll get through this together."

No sooner did Lord Celt hop down from the stage than a distant uproar reached their ears from the south. The crowd tensed up, turning toward the sound. Celt looked to Sulla, who furrowed his brow.

"My clan is camped outside the gate. There must be trouble afoot."

The six of them hurried to the south gate, the crowd trailing behind them. A guard drew up the portcullis just in time for the leaders to marshal through.

In the field outside the gate stood a hundred RoMANs, weapons at the ready. They were facing just as many Bleakers, equally eager to fight.

CHAPTER 21
DROP OUT

"Are you crazy?" a Bleaker named DreddPirate-Robi shouted at the RoMAN line. "Lower your weapons! We don't come back from kills now—do you want to murder people for real?"

Sulla stormed forward, unsheathing his Slaked Sword. "Robi—Stand down! You are outnumbered and in no position to give orders!"

The pirate turned to face Sulla. "No kidding I'm outnumbered—you wiped out the rest of my clan! I don't know what kinda voodoo you found in that cave, but you're gonna pay! As soon as I find out what you psychos did to us, you're all gonna be banned!"

Unable to stay out of this one, Lord Starr surged forward. "What we did to *you*? We lost thirty guys to that freezing thing, plus none of our dead have respawned!"

A RoMAN legionary raised his spear and his voice.

"All our NPCs are gone!"

Kit flailed her arms. "We can't log out of the game!"

"Enough!" Flames and lightning scorched the sky above General Sulla's raised sword. He gnashed his teeth and glared at the Bleakers. "Where is Jake? That coward is behind all of this, and he's the one who needs to pay."

DreddPirateRobi's shoulders sank. "Don't play games, General. You raided our city. You took Jake."

Sulla's voice was quiet but hard as steel. "If I had Jake, I'd be wearing his head around my neck right now."

A tense silence fell upon the field. A crow cawed overhead, and some thunder rumbled far off.

The pirate turned to his own people but spoke loud enough for all to hear. "So where is he?"

Lord Celt stepped into the space between the three groups. "Add that to the growing list of questions." He looked to each clan in turn as he spoke. "I know there is bad blood here, and none of us are too keen on burying hatchets anywhere other than in each other's backs right now. But, we won't get anywhere fighting with each other. We're all looking for answers; we'd get more satisfaction out of solving this big problem rather than disputing old beef."

He put an arm around Lord Starr's shoulders and drew him forward. "We're putting together an investigation into this turn of events. Lord Starr is looking for eyewitnesses from each clan, and from each of our towns, to try to piece together this mess. If you saw something you want to add to our collective knowledge, let him know."

Eyes shifted around to other clans, weapons swayed at people's sides, and a dissatisfied murmur bubbled up from all around.

A lopsided Bleaker with five teeth in his skull scuffed forward. "Why should your clan be in charge of the investigation?"

The RoMAN legionary with the spear jabbed the air in Bleak Clan's direction. "You think we'd get any honest answers with you in charge?"

CuddlyMooMoo waddled forth, almost capsizing from the weight of his axe. "I can't say I'd trust any of ya farther than I can throw ya!"

"And how far would that be, Kool-Aid Man?"

"Oh, like you're one to talk—you look like you brush your teeth with a rock!"

Lord Starr waded into the middle of the converging hordes and held his arms out. "Stop! Stop! We can't—STOP!" The groups stopped advancing, but the menace didn't vacate their eyes. "I am happy to work with someone from each clan to conduct these investigations. You might have great questions that I wouldn't have thought to ask or insights I wouldn't dream of. This isn't a me effort, it's an us effort."

The pressure valve for the entire gathering hissed as the tension slowly drained from the air. Lord Starr focused on making his breath sound steady and calm. "Is there anyone from RoME, and from Bleak, that wants to work with me on this?"

Each clan seemed to look toward the same few people in their ranks. A RoMAN praetorian, compact and severe, stepped forward first. "I will serve."

Everyone's attention shifted to the Bleak Clan, where several unkempt men endured nudges and urgings with distrusting glares. Finally, DreddPirate-Robi shambled forth, straightening a bit to appear more respectable. "Aye."

The RoMAN walked over to Lord Starr and saluted him. Lord Starr returned the courtesy. Looking around and then rasping a sigh, the Bleaker wiped a hand on his pants and advanced. Lord Starr stepped forward to meet him. Before they touched, Lord Starr dropped to the ground at the pirate's feet.

CHAPTER 22
EYE-OPENING

When Everett came to, his shoulder throbbed and he tasted blood. His spotty ceiling swirled overhead, and his ears were ringing. Freeing his left leg from under the chair he had been sitting on, he sat up and took a breath.

His arm was tangled in the Interface cord. He yanked it free from the headset, half-expecting the world to vanish or his heart to stop. Nothing happened. He was fine...sort of.

The box for the Interface reminded him that he needed to pack the whole thing up before his mom got home. He also needed to check on Alex and call Kit. What to do first?

He put his phone on speaker and called Kit while he went downstairs. It rang and rang. No answer. He fired off a text—*Call me!!!!*—before vaulting onto his bike and tearing across town.

After twenty breathless minutes, his chest ached

and his legs were overdone pasta. He dumped his bike in his dad's front yard and raced over to Alex's house.

After several knocks, Alex's mom came to the door. She beamed when she saw him. "Everett! Your mom told me you stayed home sick?" She looked past him to see if Everett's mom was parked outside. Her eyes returned to Everett, the smile fading. "Is everything all right? Does she know you're here?"

"Yeah, I did, and no she doesn't—it's really complicated." He rolled his hand and played up his effort to regain his breath. "I can call her right now if you want, but I really need to see Alex. Like right away. Please."

Everett had known Mrs. Pucello since before he could remember. He could not remember ever seeing her try so hard to not look freaked out. She eventually blinked, the corners of her mouth rising almost mechanically. "Of course, honey. How about you come on in?"

She stepped aside. Everett nodded his thanks as he entered the foyer. He looked up the steps expectantly.

"You can go on up—he's probably still plugged into that game."

Everett rested a hand on the banister and halted. "Um, so have you talked to Alex lately? Has he been down since this morning?"

Alex's mom closed the door as her eyes rolled back to search her memory. "Not for a few hours, I don't think. Weren't you online earlier, playing with him?"

Everett bounced his foot on the first step. "Maybe you should come up with me."

Mrs. Pucello tucked her hair behind her ear. Worry fluttered across her eyes, but she chased it away with a tight grin. "Sure."

They filed up the creaky steps and turned left at the top. Alex's door was at the end of the hall, the same Arctic Monkeys poster hanging there since fourth grade. Everett moved to allow Alex's mom to go first. She walked down the hall and rapped on the door.

"Alex? Alex, honey?" She turned her right ear toward the door and looked back at Everett. The worry was back.

She gripped the handle and opened the door. Everett stepped forward and leaned around her. Her hand went to her mouth, too slowly to stop the gasp from escaping.

In his black rolling chair, Alex lay slumped to his side, his hair over his face. The cord to the Interface strained from the gaming system to the back of his head, twisting his neck at an unnatural angle.

The next few moments unfolded like they were underwater. Mrs. Pucello swam over to Alex, dropping to her knees at his feet. She shook him by the shoulders, once, twice. His head lolled back and forth, limp. She reached for the Interface cord, gripping it just behind Alex's ear. The veins in her hand nearly jumped out of her skin. Before Everett could even think to speak, she pulled it free. Alex dropped to the floor.

CHAPTER 23
CONTACT

Alex's chest rose and sank, rose and sank, in rhythm with the ventilator. Tubes and wires snaked into his arms, up his nose. Drool glistened on the corner of his mouth.

Mrs. Pucello stroked Alex's forehead, her eyebrows drawn together. "Everett is here, Alex. We're here for you, honey, OK?" The sunlight through the hospital room window made her gray hairs stand out more than usual from her black hair and deepened the shadows in her crow's feet.

Everett cleared his throat. "Yeah, buddy, I'm right here. We're gonna figure this out, OK? You'll be back in no time." His stockpile of reassurances ran dry, so he fell silent again.

Everett's dad knocked lightly on the open door. Alex's mom gave him a pained smile. He walked over to Everett and drew his head to his side. "Did the doctors say anything?"

Alex's mom emitted something between a laugh and a cough. "Not really. They said there's no physical explanation for this...his brain is—what did they call it? Dormant. They said he could just—" she snapped her fingers "—and come to. Or not..."

Twenty minutes later, Everett sat in the back seat of his dad's SUV on their way to his house. Everett looked at his phone the whole time, trying to reach anyone who played *Realms*. He felt his dad's eyes on him in the rearview, but Everett didn't want to talk to him right now. He didn't want his dad's pity, but he also knew a storm was brewing behind those tired eyes.

"I'm glad you called me, bud."

"Yeh."

"Did you get ahold of your mom yet?" No response. "Ev, did you—?"

"I texted her. She's probably still at church."

The next few moments passed in tense silence. Everett stared at his screen, trying to will a response from someone. He had sent a dozen texts, Snaps, and Kiks; nothing. He wished he knew where Kit lived, her real name, *anything* that would give him a way to reach her. To go to her if he could.

His phone vibrated in his hand—Baneblade. Starr – glad to hear from u. We're all wondering where u went...u guys just disappeared mid-fight. Connection issues?

Everett didn't know where to begin. u could say that. somehow a bunch of us got trapped in-game. im the only one so far that can log out. its crazy in there. worse out here, tho. just saw wolfgang @ hospital.

They turned onto his dad's road. Everett braced himself against the door, feeling a little nauseated.

Wow...so sorry. Because of the game?

Everett replied with a nodding emoji.

Baneblade responded with a tear-shedding emoji.

Everett looked away, blinking rapidly. He took a breath and then his thumbs went back to work.

So u can jump in and out?

Yeah...I still use VR. Lotta weirdness here 2.

Like what?

The SUV crept up the driveway and idled to a stop. His dad looked back and held out one hand.

Everett sighed and handed over his phone. "Yes, warden." That convo would have to wait.

CHAPTER 24
WIRED

When Everett's dad opened the door, his ex-wife had a preemptive scowl on her face.

"Not now, Mike," Everett's mom said, holding a hand toward Mr. Starner's face as she walked into the house. She dropped Everett's traveling duffel bag by the stairs with a huff.

Everett's dad closed the door and shook his head. "We do need to talk about this, Janet."

She stopped and pivoted, taking a breath. "I know, I just—I don't want to get into a whole thing..."

"We're not," he assured her. "I just want to know if he was telling me the truth when he said you left him home alone while he was sick—"

"Oh, here we go," Everett's mom said, raising her arms and her voice. "He was fine until this morning. I was getting ready for church, and he said he had a migraine—"

"Then you call me and I'll come get him—"

"I figured you were too busy with your 'friend'—"

"Guys, please! Can you not?"

Everett's mom and dad looked toward his voice. They reluctantly made eye contact, then walked into the family room.

They found Everett slumped in a chair, staring at the TV. There was a clean-cut news anchor on screen, delivering some "Breaking News."

"—developers of the Interface, the latest trend in video gaming, are facing some serious charges. Reports started coming in this morning that some users have suddenly become comatose when disconnecting from the device, with no clear explanation why.

"The Interface, a gaming accessory that attaches to the user's head and transmits images, sounds, and even sensations directly into the player's brain, has undergone multiple rounds of testing, with no previous results of this nature. It appears that the only users affected so far were playing the wildly popular online game, *Realms of Glory*. Users playing the game without the Interface have not reported any problems."

A representative of DeepDelve Gaming flashed up on the screen, providing an official statement from the company. "We are deeply saddened by the experiences some of our users have recently had while using the Interface. Our tech team is working very hard to isolate the connection, if any, that our product may have had with these events. We are working closely with the developers of *Realms of Glory* to find answers to this obviously very concerning turn of events.

"The Interface has not caused any issues with the other games it connects with, and at this time, there are no intentions of recalling products or disrupting service for the many users who enjoy—"

Everett shut off the TV and continued to stare at the empty screen. His dad walked up behind him and lightly grabbed his shoulders.

"Hey, bud...are you OK?"

"I don't know...I mean, I'm fine. But Alex...I tried to help—" His voice caught, and a tear trailed down his cheek.

His mom sat beside him and rubbed his knee. "Do you want to talk about what happened?"

Everett cleared his throat and wiped his nose with his forearm. "Yeah, I do, but I need—there's a couple things I should do first." He looked down at his hands, fidgeting with the hem of his shirt. "There are some things I need to tell you."

His dad came around to the couch, everyone leaning forward on their knees. Everett told them everything, from finding the Interface to The General, all the way to his pirate-handshake-collapse. His parents rode the rollercoaster with him, although their emotions didn't always match his (they were pretty ticked about the whole migraine and Interface thing, unsurprisingly).

Everett gestured toward his phone, which resided in his dad's shirt pocket. "So I was trying to get ahold of anyone else I know who's still—I dunno, trapped in there. I don't know if pulling the plug out makes a difference, but it certainly doesn't help. And I want to figure out what caused all this, before I..." He swallowed. "Before I go back in."

His mom stiffened instantly, and his dad put a hand over hers to keep them from flying up. All of Dad's features hardened, but he fought to keep his voice calm. "Everett...you're not 'going back in' there. You are not playing that game—or any game like it—ever again."

Everett shot to his feet, his hands clenched at his side. "I have to! I can't let my friends all end up like Alex!"

Mom was less restrained. "Everett, you could kill yourself! We have no idea what's going on here, and with your condition, you're lucky you made it out!"

"I probably made it out *because* of my condition, Mom! Nobody else can log out, no matter how hard they try. They're all stuck in there, but I must've—I can do this."

Dad tried the "good cop" approach, adopting a

soothing tone. "Ev, I know you want to help your friends, but this isn't the way. We can contact this gaming company—call the news..."

"That's stupid! My friends could end up like Alex by then! I have to call them and—"

"Everett Lee Starner, you do not talk back in this house! You've already lost your phone for the night—"

"It's not your house, Mom, you don't get to tell me what I can or can't do here—"

Everett's dad stood up. "Both of you, stop!" His shout seemed to ring in the air for the next few seconds. He put a hand on his hip and rubbed his eyes with the other. "Everett, go to your room. Your mother and I need to discuss what to do about this, and we will call you down when we've made a decision."

"Gladly!" Everett stormed out of the room.

Everett headed upstairs, pausing only to grab his duffel bag in the hallway. It was satisfyingly heavy; the VR gear was still in there.

Everett strained his ears as he climbed the steps, relieved perhaps for the first time in his life by the sound of his parents continuing to argue.

CHAPTER 25
LAST MAN STANDING

Lord Starr stood in the middle of a lush, sun-kissed valley nestled between rolling forested hills. According to his map, he was about a mile southwest of Lordz Landing, roughly in the direction of RoME.

He checked himself over. His weapons were the same great gear, and his inventory hadn't changed. Although things looked grainier than they had on the Interface, the world seemed brighter than before. He kept his status set to "hidden" for now, just so he didn't get swarmed with messages from other players. Keeping one ear out for his parents, he set off to the northeast at a brisk pace.

The ground sloped up as he trekked along, and as the scenery scrolled by, he kept his eyes peeled for any cool wildlife. He remembered these woods had some really rare beasts that dropped cool craftable items, so if he could tag an owlbear or take down a six-legged mountain moose on his way to saving his clan, all the better.

About ten minutes in, though, he realized he hadn't heard anything, in-game or otherwise. He scanned the skies. No birds. Not a butterfly or cloud of gnats anywhere. He passed a stream. If there were frogs or fish in it, he couldn't spot any. The sun continued to shine down on him, but a chill tightened around his scalp.

Cresting the last hill, Everett paused. Lordz Landing stood in the distance, the uneven field in between. Not only were none of the clans gathered there anymore, but there was also no sign that hundreds of people had recently been there.

The reinforced walls of his town intimidated him even though he knew he was welcome to pass through them. The clan flags, a gold sword and crown on a blue background, flapped in the breeze, but otherwise the ramparts were still. Where was everyone?

He took off across the plain, his Crystal Sword flashing with each pump of his arms. It was strange to hear the clang of his armor but not feel the weight of it, although he wasn't complaining. The town grew larger with each stride, the south gate gaping open.

He began to sweat. He risked turning on his mic. "Hello? Hello?" No one answered from the walls as he approached the gate.

He made straight for the Square. "Hello?!" When he passed the inn, he skidded to a stop. The wagon stage still stood by the town hall. His new manor stared back at him from across the way. Everything looked exactly as it did an hour ago. There just weren't any people around.

His sword tip touched the ground as his arm went limp at his side. The clang of his shield against the cobblestones barely registered. His head felt like it was full of bees. He wanted to scream, but he knew his parents would race into his room right away, so he stifled an awful moan.

He drifted through the town like a ghost, seeing but not seeing anything. Every street was like a painting rather than a real place, every barrel and horseshoe and leaf just a prop left behind after a traveling performance. He messaged his friends, the clan, the entire game—it was like shouting down a well. Nothing but his own voice, hollow and then gone.

He stared at the Shieldbreaker Monument. No one was there. He saw half a dozen of his clan members still as statues there just that morning. Was everyone back to normal? Was he—was he dead? He heard only the breeze through the rooftops, and it didn't offer any answers.

A distant jingle shattered the silence. Lord Starr looked around for the source—the bakery? That dark alley? Someone behind him?

Then Everett heard footsteps on the stairs outside his room. The jingle grew louder. A green light pulsed in the periphery of his vision.

A private message.

Half relieved but still freaked out, Everett opened it.

That u starnerd?

It was Jeff Wenger. What did he want?

what jeff?

"please any1—u still jacked in? we got trapped – I need 2 know if ur ok!"

Everett's face burned. He wanted to rip off his headset and throw it against the wall.

Cmon dude why so serious? U have to come over.

y so u can do this in person? no thanx

we have a ss project together remember? Due tomorrow. Tick tock...

Everett just wanted this to end. cant. grounded

Fine my mom will call ur mom. im not gettin an f cuz of u

Whatever.

Everett growled and flung his VR gear on the bed. For the first time in his life, he wished that there was something more severe than "grounded."

CHAPTER 26
DUPLICITY

"So you waited until Sunday afternoon to figure this out?" Everett's mom charted new territories of rage over the next several minutes. He said nothing, partially mad at himself for forgetting about the project, and partially gut-sick at the thought of doing anything with Jeff Wenger.

The only thing that spared Everett's eardrums was his mom's phone warbling nonstop. She finally checked it, cursing. "Of course," she huffed, putting her hand on her forehead. "My client needs to find a notary *today* or risk losing their—it doesn't matter. Point is, I have to go. I guess you're not the only one who waits until the last minute to get things done."

She gathered her things and squeezed past Everett at the door. "Do whatever you want with him, Mike. He's your kid now."

After watching his mom pull out, Everett faced his

dad. The stare-down was painful. His dad eventually held forth Everett's phone but pulled it back when Everett reached for it. "When I call, you answer. You do your work and come right back home. If I don't hear from you in one hour, I will hunt you down."

"Yes, sir."

His dad held the phone forth again but kept a grip on it when Everett clutched it. "And no games." Everett simply nodded. His dad released.

Everett saddled up on his ten-speed and wobbled down the driveway. He used to ride his bike all the time when he was younger, but he was rusty now, to say the least. Once he cleared the mailbox by mere centimeters, he was zigzagging down the street, trying to mentally rehearse how to brake without flying over the handlebars.

Nine breathless minutes later, he dumped his bike on Jeff's front yard, near four or five others. His legs felt like noodles as he made for the door. Before he could ring the bell, the door swung open. Jeff and a few of his pals smirked from the doorway.

"Look who it is: the man of the hour! Get in here. C'mon guys, move!" Jeff pushed his friends back to make room for Everett. When he entered, his face hurt already from the strained smile. His left eyelid twitched. His torso was filled with Pop Rocks. *This was a good idea.*

As they ushered Everett toward the basement, Jeff

and his friends asked Everett questions faster than he could think.

"So are you really a Lord?"

"What the heck happened with the Bleak clan?"

"Do you know The General?"

"Does it suck to get raided so hard?"

They tramped down the stairs and turned right at the bottom. Everett stopped when he saw Jeff's gaming set-up. Half the basement was a giant room, and that room had a projection screen that basically took up an entire wall. He had six wireless Interface headsets on stands by the stairway, with a dedicated console for each one. There were all kinds of crazy ergo-style chairs and bean bags to lounge on, and Jeff's friends gravitated toward their favorites.

"Wait a minute," Everett said, a stone growing in his stomach. "I thought we were just working on social studies? I can't play games right now."

Jeff's right-hand man, Brayden, sat forward in his bean bag chair. "You're kidding, right? Dude, you gotta show us your whacked-out server!"

Everett's brow furrowed. "What do you mean?"

Odell, a gigantic ninth grader, leaned back and pointed. "Waitwaitwait—he doesn't know!" He let out a high-pitched laugh. "Your whole clan is like—J, show 'im!"

Jeff got up and retrieved a chrome yellow headset from its stand. Everett held up his hands defensively.

"Seriously, I promised my parents I wouldn't play after what happened with Alex—"

Jeff shook his head and wrapped the molded plastic around his skull. "Don't worry, Star-nerd...we don't want you upsetting Mommy and Daddy." He picked up a massive remote and pointed it at the projector on the ceiling. Then he pressed the red button behind his left ear, turning on the Interface. Suddenly, the screen on the wall displayed exactly what Jeff was seeing in his mind.

On-screen, Jeff (KidFleek, apparently) exited his town's inn and hurried through the Square. By the looks of it, he belonged to Camelot Clan, not too far from Lordz Landing. He hopped on a tan courser and galloped to Everett's town in a few minutes. The rolling landscape, the wind in the horse's mane, sunlight showing through a passing butterfly's wing—everything looked so real, it was like looking through a window rather than at a screen.

Everett tried to keep his mouth closed. It would be super uncool to act impressed with this. "How does that—?"

Seth grabbed his shoulder and shook it playfully. "It's some crazy tech his dad rigged up. Now we can all be lucky enough to see the world through Jeff's eyes."

"I can still hear you toolbags," Jeff said, his eyes rolling around under his eyelids like he was having a frenetic dream. In-game, he rode up to the gate of Lordz Landing—which was closed. "Hey! Let me in!"

Everett sat forward. "That's not going to—"

"Coming, sir!" A moment later, an NPC peered over the ramparts. "Welcome, KidFleek!" The portcullis ratcheted up and Jeff's avatar trotted right in.

Everett's eyes went wide, and his mouth couldn't resist hiking up its corners. The NPCs were manning their shops, walking the streets, working on the construction in the west end. All throughout town, his fellow clan members milled around; he recognized a few names, but none of the people he left behind were here.

"They're all here..." Everett noticed Jeff's friends staring at him, so he tried playing it off. "That's my new manor over there, right on the Square."

Brayden hit Jeff in the arm with the back of his hand. "Yo, talk to the townspeople!" Odell and Seth seconded the idea.

Jeff laughed. He was looking at the ceiling, but he tilted his ear toward Everett. "What's your gamertag again?"

"It's, uh, Lord Starr now."

"Oh, Your Majesty—I didn't realize." Jeff did a fancy bow. Earning a chuckle, he refocused on the game.

KidFleek dismounted and approached a woman

carrying a basket of bread through the Square. "Good day, milady."

"Good morrow, sirrah. Can I help you?"

"Yes, please. Can you tell me where Lord Starr is?"

The woman's face contorted. Her eyes rolled all around in her skull. Her limbs began to twitch. "I I I does not register Lord Starr to me to me to me to me..."

The other boys lost it. Everett laughed along but felt sick in his heart. "What if you ask another player?"

Odell covered his mouth. "You really don't know, do you?"

Jeff's avatar ran over to AgentSquad15, a half-lizard ranger that Everett remembered doing a few quests with about a month ago. "AgentSquad! You're even uglier than your mom!"

The Jeff fans cackled. KidFleek stood right in front of AgentSquad and jabbed at his face with a spear. AgentSquad just walked by, unfazed.

"Do the thing with the—!"

"Yeah, make him—!"

"All right, all right!" Jeff waved his arms around. KidFleek threw down his weapon and shield. He chucked pieces of his armor around the Square. He smashed a flask of Dragon Water on his head and did the chicken dance. A few NPCs gathered around and began to clap, but the players just kept going about their business.

Odell and Brayden almost fell out of their chairs. Seth was practically crying. Jeff continued flapping his elbows and making circles around the room.

Everett stood and flung his arm out. "What are you, invisible? What the heck?!"

"It's like I'm not even here...watch!" KidFleek grabbed his gear, re-equipped it, and entered the Warehouse. He helped himself to about thirty thousand gold coins, a few mythic relics, and the Demon Scythe off a guard's back. Lordz Clan members just milled about, oblivious.

Jeff held up a hand toward his captive audience. "OK, now watch what happens when I go to Bleak Island."

Jeff left town, hopped on a boat, and sailed across The Restless Sea. Over the next ten minutes, the other boys talked about their weekends, cracked inside jokes, and checked their phones.

Everett sank back in his seat and reread his messages just to look preoccupied, but he kept one eye on the screen. The ocean was growing foggy, and the surf kicked up pretty hard. Jeff was getting close to the island.

Through a misty veil, the ominous bulk of the Bleaker's fortress emerged. A dull red glow pulsed through the haze in certain spots. It wasn't foggy...that was smoke. The fortress was still burning.

Jeff's avatar beached his boat and scrambled

through the wreckage that used to be the front gate. When KidFleek entered the fort, Everett's stomach lurched forward.

Most of the buildings were ruined, and those still standing burned. As long as they burned, though, nothing changed; they didn't collapse or get worse, the fire just danced in place. Beneath the smoke and falling fire, there were piles of dead Bleakers, RoMANS, and Lordz. Swarms of players rummaged through the bodies, taking OP weapons and armor. Strangely, when a body had its weapon taken, the next person could take that same weapon. It was like every corpse was an endless repository of items, and opportunists were all over it.

KidFleek fleeced a high-ranking RoMAN over and over, collecting a half-dozen Wraith Lances and a full set of Adamant Armor. Jeff laughed. "That's goin' in my Ferrari fund!"

He hit a few more bodies, trying to avoid the crowds. Down a dim alley, he stumbled upon a lone body. There was a distinctive symbol on his back, a sword and crown. "Hey, Ev, you know this guy?" KidFleek searched the corpse and liberated a giant glowing spear. Gungnir.

"Whoa," Seth, Brayden, and Odell said in concert.

The room went bleary and began to spin. Everett grabbed for a shelf to keep from tipping over. Seth caught him under the arm before he toppled. "Dude?

What's wrong?"

Everett rocked to his feet and shook his arm free. "I gotta go."

He was up the steps and out the door before Jeff could even remove his headset. Everett rode away so fast that the wind swept his tears away almost as quickly as he shed them.

By the time he realized he was headed to his mom's house, he was practically there.

CHAPTER 27
GET OUT

Everett sat on the front porch of his mom's, arms dangling off his knees, head hanging forward. His legs tried to bounce away his frustration, but it remained. The sun still hung in the sky, low behind the trees across the street, but it felt like it should be midnight.

What are you doing? he said to himself. *Do you want to be in trouble? You're already grounded until—and for a game?*

But it's not a game anymore. You saw what happened to Alex. And all your friends are still in there. Kit is still in there.

And what are you going to do about it? Ruin your real life for a virtual one? Mom and Dad said to deal with this from the outside. It's obviously not safe in the game—clowns like Jeff will make sure of that.

Somewhere far off, the sky rumbled. Dark clouds began to gather above the trees. Everett dug around for the spare house key under the flowerpots and got inside just before fat drops of water splattered on the sidewalk. He looked outside at his capsized bike getting soaked in the yard. *No point dragging it inside now.*

He looked around the dim house, a dull dread spreading in his chest. He'd lived in this house his whole life, but it still looked unfamiliar with the lights out. He flicked on the living room lights to cast off some of the gloom, but being alone kept the worry draped over his heart.

Everett retreated to his room and closed the door. He stared at his phone, unsure of his next move. He wished someone would just call or text so he didn't have to decide.

He sent out a few snaps to friends just to fish for something, and when he heard nothing back, he bit the bullet and texted his dad. Wasn't thinking—rode to moms. Raining. Can u get me?

For the next few agonizing seconds, the blank face of his phone glowed back at him. Then a buzz.

New Message From Kit.

His heart fluttered as he touched the pop-up.

this is Kates mom who is this i found her in her room not answering saw your message dont unplug her what do you want what did you do to her??????

Everett's mouth dried out instantly, and his arms tingled. He tapped "reply" but couldn't think of what to say. After a few attempts, he sent this:

I'm Everett, Kate's friend. We play online together with another friend of mine. That other friend just went to the hospital when his mom unplugged him. I don't know what's going on, but I don't want that to happen to Kate. Can u please let me try to help her first?

His legs bounced as he waited for a response. One minute. Two minutes. Finally, his phone dinged again.

ohmygod should i call 911 what can you do please help!!!

Another text: his mom. Where are you? Jeff's mom said you left 20 minutes ago?

His dad. Everett — Call us now!

"Kit". What should I do???

Everett closed his eyes to try to put the brakes on the carousel of thoughts whirling around his mind. *I can't handle this. This isn't happening. I'm going to wake up and this will all be a terrible dream.*

When he opened his eyes, his room looked otherworldly. His bed, sulking beneath a mass of twisted covers, looked like a pile of his fallen clanmates. The glowing nest of chargers plugged in the corner pulsed like the distant fires of the burning Bleaker Island. The hockey poster hanging by his closet became a grim-faced plunderer, scythe raised and ready to strike. And by the door sat a ghostly treasure chest of promise, the boxed-up Interface.

He picked up his phone. He tapped "reply." Don't worry. I'll get her out.

CHAPTER 28
ONE BY ONE...

"What did you do?!"

"I don't know, I just went to shake his hand—!"

"Back off, just—everybody, stop!"

Lord Forlani stood between a horde of angry RoMANs, murderous Bleakers, and triggered Lordz, miraculously keeping the three groups from slaughtering each other.

Kit rushed into the middle of the fray. She knelt beside Lord Starr and looked him over. Her face tightened. "Zero! Can you—I don't know, just do something!"

The three groups parted like the Red Sea as the floating mage drifted toward the center. She stopped by Kit and raised her glowing fists. Her eyes pulsed green as she surveyed Lord Starr's fallen body. The glow faded from her hands and face, and she turned to the crowd.

"He is simply gone, like the others. The Bleaker had no hand in this."

General Sulla looked like he just swallowed some bile. "Maybe not that Bleaker, but there is one Bleaker behind this, and we're all just standing around waiting for the next person to drop!"

Kit stood and put a hand on his chest. "Please...can we just get him back in town? He might come back, right?" Her eyes glistened beneath drawn-together brows.

Sulla grunted. He sheathed his sword and swelled out his chest. "You can stand around and play Clue all day if you want...I'm going to hunt down that snake with or without you." He slung Lord Starr over one shoulder and began walking back toward Lordz Landing.

Kit looked from the RoMANs to the Bleakers, a pained expression on her face. "This isn't what Ev— what Lord Starr would want. We need to work together to get out of this mess." She pointed toward his receding form. "That could have been any one of us...and it might soon be unless we do something to stop this."

The assemblage shifted and murmured, avoiding eye contact.

Lord Celt walked up behind Kit and put a hand on her shoulder. "Let us handle this. You should go be with Lord Starr."

Kit reluctantly nodded and made for the town. Zero and Lord Forlani escorted her, along with many of the other Lordz Clan members. A contingent of RoMANs followed suit, apparently considering Sulla their key into the city.

No one thought much of this, but when a Bleak Clan member broke from his ranks, RoMANs and Lordz readied their weapons. The Bleaker, a handsome, olive-skinned Sikh in traditional white garb, stopped in his tracks and held forth his hands.

"Please—I mean no harm. That Lord, he was just a boy, right? Most of you are just boys, children playing a game.

"I am a father, trapped here away from my family. A real person, like all of you. This clan I joined just for fun. Things are different now. I just want to help that boy, if I can."

Lord Celt weighed the man's words with his eyes. He gestured toward the town with a tilt of his head.

The man put his hands together and bowed his head. "Thank you, sir." He faced the crowd one last time. "Remember, we are all in this together. We are not true enemies; we have only pretended to be."

As the man hurried to catch up with the procession, those remaining on the field shifted their attention to Lord Celt. Resigned to the fact that he was in charge here now, Celt put his fists on his hips. "So...anyone know a good trust-building exercise?"

***

Kit stayed within arm's reach of Lord Starr's body the entire time they marched down to Lordz Landing and into the Square. She kept trying to read Sulla's face, but it was a mask of warring sentiments, rage and confusion and not a little concern.

When they came close to the wagon stage, Kit took Sulla by the elbow. "Lay him on this...I want people to be able to always have an eye on him in case he comes to."

General Sulla gently placed the body on the wagon. He shook his head at it. "He's not going to— nobody has come back from this." His features consolidated into a single emotion: pity. "I'm sorry."

A small crowd began to form around them, respectful but eager to see Lord Starr. They quietly looked him over, wringing their hands and whispering condolences. A Valkyrie placed her hand on the small of Kit's back, and Kit leaned into her shoulder.

Just as the Square reached its most somber tone, a shout fractured the silence. A dull roar, like the ocean from afar, swelled in the distance. The ground rumbled as the noise grew closer. Someone was shouting, but they couldn't tell who. "Let us through, then close the gates!"

The thunder of the portcullis slamming shut shook the ground. Lord Celt came racing into the

Square, with about fifty clan members in tow. "Forlani—collapsed!" he gasped. "A Bleaker and two RoMANs just dropped—it's chaos!"

Sulla surged toward him. "You left my men out there with those—maniacs?" He stood a few inches from Celt's face, the cords standing out in his neck.

"*You* left your men out there," Lord Celt replied calmly. "You're welcome to join them if you dislike the safety of our walls."

Steel clamored against the town walls and arrows began to clatter and thunk against the rooftops. Zero's fists flashed red as she floated to the center of the Square and raised her arms.

Kit grabbed a handful of her cloak. "Zero, no! Protect us from them, but don't hurt anyone...please!"

From the shadowy recesses of her hood, Zero's eyes cycled from red to green to blue. "Very well." Lightning jumped from her outstretched hands into the sky. A crackling blue net wove through the air, above the rooftops. Arrows and spells deflected off it, or impacted and sizzled away.

"Awesome—thank you!" Kit hugged her. They retreated toward the wagon, where CuddlyMooMoo and some other clan members now gathered. Kit glanced toward Celt and Sulla, who continued their staring contest, then looked back at the wagon crowd. "We have to get away from here. We're safe for now, but if we don't move soon—"

A flaming arrow struck the wagon, right by Lord Starr's thigh. The wood began to smolder, and the fire spread toward his leg. Kit yanked the arrow out and Zero doused it with a water spell before it did any major damage, but everyone's heart jumped one step closer to cardiac arrest.

The dwarf raised his axe. "All right, you heard the lady! C'mon, let's go!" He leaned his weight into the wagon. With the help of a few other guys, he got it rolling roughly northward, toward the alley between the Warehouse and the Stables.

As they gained momentum, everyone was racing to keep up with the wagon. More arrows struck the street and stores around them, and balls of flame splashed on the cobblestones nearby.

"Zero, is there anything else you can do? They're shooting over your—" Kit didn't get to finish that thought, because she suddenly crumpled on the sidewalk like a rag doll.

CuddlyMooMoo dashed around the side of the cart and scooped Kit up just before the wagon wheel would have crushed her legs. He hefted her over his shoulder and barreled toward the Stables. "Get the wagon in here! C'mon!"

When the wagon hit the curb, Lord Starr's body nearly popped off. The three clan members trying to guide the runaway train were jarred off their feet, and the wagon wedged into the open doorway of the stables.

The dwarf clambered over the wagon and heaved Kit onto a pile of straw inside. The others placed Lord Starr on some hay bales nearby. CuddlyMooMoo scurried outside to prop the wagon up and better block the door. He tried to get Zero's attention, but she was busy weaving a new spell to hold off the rain of projectiles. The dwarf scampered through a side window with some help from a tall sack of oats.

Inside the stable was a grim sight. Kit and Lord Starr remained motionless in the middle of the room. The other three clan members, although outwardly broad-shouldered warriors, knelt like frightened children over them both. Two curious horses and a one-eyed goat straggled over to investigate.

The dwarf stood atop a hay bale and took in the scene, shaking his head. "It can't get much weirder than this."

Then he heard a strange sound. It started as a soft gurgling, then turned into a muffled snort. He thought one of the horses was about to sneeze, but when he looked closer, it seemed like Lord Starr's body was shifting.

Then he opened his eyes.

CHAPTER 29
RE-ENTRY

Lord Starr blinked several times, trying to make sense of what he saw. Three strange men stared down at him, eyes bugging out of their heads. A couple of horses and a dwarf in a sparkly leotard looked equally puzzled to see him. There was also a goat.

Lord Starr's mouth started to move, but nothing came out. The dwarf leaned forward, eyebrows raised. "Well, say something!"

"Why...why is my butt burning?"

CuddlyMooMoo hopped down and walked over to Lord Starr, placing a hand on his shoulder. "There's never a good answer for that question." He shooed the animals away, and the other clan members stepped back, pretending they were more interested in looking outside.

The dwarf laid down, leaned his chin on his hand,

and propped his elbow on Lord Starr's arm. "So... what's it like?"

"Hmm?"

"Coming back from the dead? Was there a light at the end of a tunnel? Did you meet five people?"

"Um, yeah, actually...but, no, I was just back with my family. I saw Alex—Wolfgang—in the...he's in a coma. I think that's what happens to everyone who freezes or dies." He propped himself up on his elbows.

"I talked with Baneblade...he seems to be fine. It's like half our clan is on one side of a curtain, and the other half—Kit!" Lord Starr sat up, toppling the dwarf. He crawled over to her and tried to shake her awake. "What happened?"

CuddlyMooMoo released a heavy sigh and swirled one hand in the air. "It was like all the others—she was talking, and then she just dropped in the middle of running in here." He placed a meaty hand gently on her forehead. "Maybe she'll snap out of it like you did."

Everett swallowed. "I doubt it. I think I'm the only one who can do that."

The dwarf squinted one eye and drew up the corner of his mouth. "Why's that? What makes you so—"

A deafening boom shook the town, knocking everyone off their feet. The support beams in the stable screamed as they leaned and strained to stay up.

Lord Starr sprang to his feet. "What was that?"

Planting the butt of his axe on the ground, CuddlyMooMoo pulled himself to his feet. "The Bleakers and RoMANs. Guess they got through the gate."

"What—Why?" Another crash shook the building, tilting the supports a few more degrees. "We have to get out of here!" He picked up Kit and made for the entrance. It wouldn't give.

"I blocked it—I thought we'd be safer..." The dwarf looked around. "Follow me!"

They rushed toward a side door, the three other clan members each leading an animal behind them. CuddlyMooMoo breached the door with a resounding stroke of his axe and the lot of them spilled out into the alleyway. The stables creaked, groaned, listed, and collapsed, sending dust and hay up in clouds.

Everyone's chests puffed in and out like bellows. The dwarf looked from one face to another with an irrepressible grin. "Aw, c'mon—you have to admit that was pretty cool!"

The tumult of two advancing armies killed some of the buzz. Lordz Clan members raised their battle cries to meet the invaders, but the swirling dust obscured the action.

Lord Starr looked over the occupants of the

alleyway. "Well, we can't just stand around here...help me with that wagon."

More and more RoMANs and Bleakers charged into the Square, fighting with and against each other as the Lordz ranks swelled. As furious as everyone seemed to be, people were obviously tempering their strokes, trying to avoid fatal contact. When someone was struck, they would howl out in real, actual pain, not the typical in-game grunts everyone was used to.

As the three clans clustered together, staring each other down, a commanding voice filled the air. "EVERYBODY, STOP!"

The clans stopped and looked toward the sound. The clatter of hoof beats and rumble of wagon wheels filled the Square. Each faction, to a man, stared at the sight: Lord Starr, standing on the wagon, with three men, a dwarf, an unconscious cat-girl, and a goat at his feet.

CHAPTER 30
RISE AND FALL

Three hundred eyes stared at him, jaws slack, still panting from the exertion of combat. A few barrels and rooftops smoldered from arrows or wizard's fire, but other than that, the Square was quiet as a crypt.

Lord Starr spread his arms to address the dumbstruck crowd. "I have been to the other side, and I am back to tell you what I saw." He knew it was overly dramatic, but in the moment, it felt right.

He stepped to the front of the wagon, clasping his hands. "I don't know how to get you out of here safely yet, but I do know what happens to anyone who collapses or dies in-game." He shared Alex's story, the audience hanging on his every word. All were moved—many wept, some from sympathy, some from fear.

After taking a moment to compose himself, he aimed one hand toward the south. "On that field, I said we need to put aside our differences and work together to solve this problem. That mission is no less urgent now. We must find out how to get everyone out of here before we all end up...gone. I will ask once more, but only once...who is with me?"

His fellow clan members offered the first smattering of support. A RoMAN raised his shield, and three others followed suit. The Sikh Bleaker pledged himself to the cause. More and more people stepped forward, until, in unison, a hundred voices shouted their assent. Lord Starr couldn't help but feel a little swept away by owning the moment.

But it was short-lived. The General approached the wagon, the crowd giving him a wide berth. He ascended to the stage, the wood and iron groaning under the immense weight of him and his armor. He stood next to Lord Starr, looking like a linebacker next to—well, a middle school boy.

The General took a deep breath, but when he spoke, it was without bluster or rage. He was disconcertingly calm. "We stay together, we die together—that's the fate this 'coalition for truth' will earn you. My men and I will sail to Bleak Island and scour every inch of it for Jake. That's your answer. That's our only hope.

"Bleak Clan, you are welcome to accompany us, and I will guarantee you safe passage. I bear no ill will toward you. Jake is the one behind this. He's the only one I'm after."

He turned and walked off the wagon, which rose six inches in his absence. Sulla continued walking toward the east gate, seemingly unconcerned with whether anyone came with him or not.

In twos and threes, the RoMANs peeled away from the crowd and ran to catch up with The General. So did a few Bleakers, surprisingly. The Lordz and those who remained watched Lord Starr for what to do next.

Lord Starr watched Sulla walking away. "General...General!" The hulk of a man stopped but did not turn. His silver cape swayed in the breeze. Lord Starr clenched and released his fists. "Now is not the time to charge into things. The risks here are real now. I've been to the other side of this, Sulla. This isn't a game anymore."

The General looked over his shoulder. "It never was."

After being momentarily impressed by the sheer coolness of that Clint Eastwood line, Lord Starr threw up his hands. "Do you really think one person could do all this?"

Sulla squinted at the sky. "With enough conviction, one person can do anything he puts his mind to." With that, he stomped a foot and resumed his march eastward.

Dazed, Lord Starr slowly looked back at the

thinning crowd in the Square. The reverence in their eyes gave way to doubt, to fear and, in some cases, to disgust. He looked down at Kit, lifeless as a scarecrow at his feet. Then he remembered to breathe.

He drew his brows together, leaned toward the crowd, and held up a hand. "I promise you, I will never put any of you in danger. If we want to leave this place, and turn our back on The General's... mission, I am with you. If you wish to surrender, end this senseless feud, and wait for what is to come, I'll wave that white flag. And if you think that sailing to that island and hunting down Jake will bring this nightmare to a quicker end, I'll captain the ship for you. I'm not going to pretend I know how to get out of this mess. But I will not drag any of you into something you don't want."

The crowd began talking, first at a simmer, then a slow boil. Lord Starr held his pose, leaning forward, his expression as earnest as a puppy. Most people tried to avoid his gaze, but it was worse when they would look at him, shake their heads, and walk away. Within a few minutes, his horde of followers shrank to little more than the occupants of the wagon.

Zero floated over and knelt by Kit, trying to comfort or revive her. Lord Celt stood near the Town Hall, accompanied by about five noobs, including the one Everett had saved from the cliff on Bleak Island. Besides that, there were a handful of Bleakers clustered by the Inn, probably deciding whether to loot the town quickly or make a run for it. A lone man, with a black beard and a turban, stood in the middle of the square, looking at Lord Starr with a mixture of respect and concern.

Lord Starr's shoulders sagged. He glanced over at CuddlyMooMoo, who was sitting on the edge of the wagon, petting the goat. He walked over next to the dwarf and crossed his arms. "What am I doing, 'breaker? Why did I think for a second that I could be a leader?"

CuddlyMooMoo tousled the goat's hair and let out a short laugh. "There's all kinds of leaders, my boy. And having the most people on your side doesn't necessarily make you right." He made his way to his feet, forcing a bleat out of the poor goat. He hopped off the wagon and waddled toward the Town Hall. "Well, what are you waiting for, Starr? Let's make our plan."

"Our plan? What can *we* possibly do? Either Sulla finds Jake and ends all this, or he doesn't, and he comes back here for us. Unless you know something I don't, there aren't any other options."

The Sikh raised a hand and walked briskly toward Lord Starr. "Actually, sir, I know something that may be of use." He stopped about ten feet from the two.

CuddlyMooMoo looked the man over, and then up at Lord Starr. Lord Starr weighed his words before responding to the Bleaker.

"And what might that be?"

The bearded man tented his fingers and tipped his head respectfully. "I know where Jake is."

CHAPTER 31
ROUGH SEAS

In the rise and fall of each wave, The General stood steadfast on the prow of his trireme, his eyes fixed on the horizon. Heavy clouds gathered overhead, blotting out the setting sun. A stiff wind blew across the decks. Drums accompanied each pull of the oars, and dozens of men chatted nervously on the top deck, but The General might as well have been alone on a tropical island, so absorbed was he by that distant shore.

A heavy-browed RoMAN named Flavius ventured to the front of the ship. He rested one hand on the hilt of his short sword and pretended he too could see what The General was staring at. "Sir, the men have been discussing what our plan is, once we reach the island. Is our goal to capture Jake, or...?" He cleared his throat. "Do you have any idea—do you know if that will fix this?"

Sulla drew Flavius close with one arm and faced the crew. "Our goal is simple: we go to Bleak Island. We hunt down Jake. I kill him. Easy like Sunday morning."

The men exchanged nervous looks, nodded, and gave their assent.

"Splendid!" Sulla shoved Flavius toward a knot of centurions standing mid-deck. "Now stop messing around—we're approaching Bleak Island."

Thick curtains of smoke hung over the water, the dull red of a dozen fires bleeding through the veil of black. Sulla grinned as the distant blazes grew closer, the smoke surrounding the ship now.

Then, the winds began to shift. The smoke rolled and coiled as the ship slowed. The sails flattened against the masts, and the deck began to list. Sulla began shouting orders, and men scrambled to change tack.

They quickly leveled out the ship, but now they were drifting away from the island. The General stomped toward the tiller, waving his arms. "Hard alee!"

The boat surged backward harder, knocking men off their feet. From the sides of the boat, the cracking of banks of oars resounded like cannons.

At once, a furious storm broke overhead, showering the trireme with sheets of rain. Lightning snaked across the sky and twice struck their mainsail, but did not ignite it. Thunder boomed with each flash, drowning out all by the most impassioned cries of the men onboard.

With a herculean effort, Sulla and four others lashed the sails to the masts and muted most of the wind's impact on the ship. The waves, however, surged and smashed against the sides with relentless fury, tossing the ship like a piece of cork.

Sulla wrapped some rigging around his arm and fought to keep his feet on the slanted, sodden deck. A fellow RoMAN, hugging the railing, stared past Sulla in horror. Sulla clenched his eyes shut and screamed. "Brace yourselves!"

A huge wave threw the ship against a rocky shoal, shearing off more oars and smashing a massive hole in the portside. Dozens of men were thrown onto the rocks, or into the sea, never to be seen again.

Sulla strained with all his might to stay onboard, his eyes staring north. The smoke was parting ahead, revealing how close—and yet how far—Bleak Island was. He cursed the seven winds, shook his sword at the gods of the sea and sky, howled his hatred to the world, but the storm swallowed every word and scattered them like dust.

The waves dragged the ship across the shoal and then tossed it back into the open sea. The deck wavered to and fro, but finally mellowed out for a moment. Then, as the hull filled with water, it listed to the portside steadily. Sulla was soon staring into the roiling abyss, all but dangling from the ropes that now ensnared his left arm.

Pulling his Slaked Sword free with one hand, The General slashed at the ropes. He cut two with the first slice but caused himself to spin haphazardly. As he steadied himself to hack the final rope, he felt the ship shudder and stop moving. Then it began pulling the other way.

"No! No! NOOOOOOOO!" a man screamed from behind him. A loud, wet sound slapped against the deck. Then another, and another. Sulla jabbed the deck with his sword to spin himself the other way, just as a fourth gigantic tentacle reached up and coiled around the foremast. Less than thirty feet below him, the maw of a giant Kraken gaped wide, just as the screaming RoMAN dropped in.

The cacophony of the storm, the dying ship, the cries of men, and the raging sea—these were a mere whisper compared to the fear and fury howling inside Sulla's head. Kicking and writhing, he fought to climb away from the creature and escape the sinking ship. Hooking his legs around the mast, he severed the last of the ropes. He pulled himself onto the spar so that he lay facing down at the awful beast.

The Kraken extended two tentacles, each as big around as wagon wheels, hungrily toward him. Sulla pushed up to his knees, then tried to balance on the quaking timber. The first tentacle latched around the wood just two feet in front of him, wrapping around and snapping it off like a breadstick.

The General managed to keep his footing, whirling his sword about to steady himself. When the second tentacle drew near, he slashed at it, but too soon. He pitched forward, flailing through the air. The monster's huge, fleshy head rose from the water to meet him, its eyes reflecting dual images of Sulla's cascading form. The impact of the freezing water knocked the breath right out of the fallen General.

In a slow but inevitable collapse, the boat bubbled into the rioting sea, tentacles embracing it like a treasured doll. One by one, the men still fighting for life disappeared below the surface.

The storm broke, the wind shifted, and the smoke no longer obscured the island. Eventually the sea returned to its former, placid rhythms. Someone passing by then would have never known the horrors that had just occurred. The only sign that anyone had just been there washed up on the shore a little later. One might mistake it for some misshapen flotsam, or a particularly large mass of wrack. Upon closer inspection, though, one would realize the shape on the coast of Bleaker Island was a man, with a silver cloak, and a massive, flame-bladed sword.

CHAPTER 32
THE WELL

They had been running through the woods for almost ten minutes now, and Lord Starr was sucking air. Lord Celt kept up fairly well, but Zero struggled to keep Kit levitating safely away from the trees while steering herself. Everyone else said to leave Kit behind, but Lord Starr wouldn't have it. In the end, his sentimentality won out.

CuddlyMooMoo had trouble with anything taller than a small tree root on account of his stubby little legs; he tended to roll with it though—often literally. The Sikh set the pace, his feet barely touching the mossy ground as he led the group.

"Hold on!" the dwarf gasped. "We're dying here."

The Sikh trotted to a stop but seemed baffled by their fatigue. "We are almost there, friends. It is worth it to push a little longer."

Lord Starr, hands on his knees, steadied his

breathing. Lord Celt stood next to him, arms akimbo, arching his back. "You're the young buck, Starr...you should be ahead of us all!" He slapped him on the back good-naturedly.

CuddlyMooMoo sauntered up to the Sikh and leaned his shoulder on a tree. "How can you be so sure Jake is...wherever you're taking us? This isn't even near your island—or anything else for that matter."

"That misconception," the Sikh said, smiling, "is exactly what makes this the perfect hiding place." He waved to everyone to follow and resumed what was, for him, a leisurely jog.

The Lordz did their best to keep up, leaping fallen tree trunks and large rocks while avoiding the ditches and puddles. They came to a steep path, and once they climbed it, the shade of the forest gave way to a bright, secluded glade. In the middle of it, almost too postcard-perfect to be believed, sat a small, cheery cottage, its little chimney puffing up gentle clouds of smoke. They all stopped and stared at the sight.

"That?" CuddlyMooMoo pointed at the cottage with his axe. "That's the hideout of the most bloodthirsty gamer in the land? The man who put this curse or poison or whatever on the lot of us? The filthy Bleaker—no offense—who executed me, is living in a Smurf house?"

The Sikh closed his eyes and held up a hand. "Jake

is not in this cottage. This merely marks where we will go to find him."

Lord Celt put his fingertips on his forehead. "I thought we just *went* to where he is!"

The Sikh took a step toward the cottage. "Please, just come. It will be clearer if I show you."

Zero drifted up next to Lord Celt. "We've come this far...we might as well look."

The group filed after the Sikh solemnly, except CuddlyMooMoo, who seemed very eager to sink his axe into something with a pulse.

As they approached the cottage, the Sikh veered away from the front door and toward the left side of the house. The others exchanged looks, but continued to follow, albeit more cautiously, and with one hand on their hilts.

They circled around to the back, past a charming little garden, and saw a stone well sitting in the middle of the fenced-in yard. The Sikh opened the little fence gate and placed a hand on the well's edge. "This, my friends, is where you will find Jake."

The dwarf leaned his axe on the ground and rested his arm on the head. "Riiiiiiiiight...um, yeah, thanks for the tip, Blackbeard...we'll jump right on in that well and find Mr. Da Rippa."

The Sikh gestured toward the mouth of the well and scanned the eyes of the men. "This is not an ordinary well. This well leads to the network of tunnels our clan uses to sneak up on and quickly escape from other clans throughout the Realms. We came this way to scout Lordz Landing after your success in the Shattered Peaks dungeon. We've struck out at RoME several times from this very well. And when your clan attacked us, Jake tried to escape into one of the many tunnels on our island.

"I say 'tried to' because he did not make it very far down the tunnel when he froze—like so many did when that blue flash struck. Our clan has been guarding his location since then, desperate to find out what your people, or the RoMANs, had done. It seems clear now that whatever this is, it was not wrought by any of us."

His eyes grew intense—not with anger or fear, but with gravity. He held forth one trembling hand. "I have led you here. I can take you directly to Jake, without a single Bleaker or trap or other sort of trick along the way. I will do that for you. But know this: I will not stand by and watch you slay a man before you've at least talked to him. Are we clear?"

The four Lordz faced each other, pictures of distrust and uncertainty. Ultimately, everyone else's eyes settled on Lord Starr. CuddlyMooMoo grinned at him.

Lord Starr raised one eyebrow and looked to the Sikh. "We are clear. Lead the way."

The Sikh nodded and produced five Glowstone

necklaces. He gave each of them one to wear, putting the last one on himself. Then he leaped in the well, trusting them to follow. They did.

CHAPTER 33
BURIED

Down, down, down Lord Starr slid, quickly discovering that the well was not so much a vertical shaft in the ground as a gradual slope that sent him careening into the darkness, like a slime-coated waterslide. He caught flashes of the Sikh's glowing necklace, but mostly he stared into darkness, and while he thought passingly of how abruptly this might end, he mostly focused on how freakin' awesome this was.

"Almost there!" the Sikh said, followed by the grunt of his impact at the bottom.

"Look out below!" Lord Starr said, plunging from the mouth of the tunnel and onto a thick mat of reeds just a few feet from the Sikh. He laid on his back a moment, laughing at the thrill of it all, but the shrieks of CuddlyMooMoo and Lord Celt chased him out of the way. The two hit the mat in close succession, with

Zero gliding out last, and Kit hovering behind in a soft green glow.

Everyone soon found their feet and regrouped at the end of the tall but claustrophobic chamber they found themselves in. The Sikh ducked his head to enter the only corridor leading out of the room and looked back at the others.

"I promised you I would bring you to Jake. Please do not forget your promise to me." The Lordz exchanged looks and nodded to him. He waved them along. "Let's go."

The next thirty minutes involved neck-cramping shuffles down winding tunnels, perilous crossings over bottomless gaps, and treks up and down stairways so steep and narrow it was, at times, like tiptoeing on pool cues. When they reached the first space bigger than a phone booth, they stretched their aching limbs and backs with many a groan.

"Are we at all close to...wherever we're going right now?" Lord Celt said between stretches.

The Sikh surveyed the area, a dim, rocky room that looked like every other place they'd seen so far down here. He narrowed his eyes and sniffed the air. "We are beneath the Restless Sea, not far from an island inhabited by a scrappy little clan called the FunEshuns. We hit them up from time to time, but we sort of respect their lively spirit and tend to give them a pass."

He pulled a canteen from inside his shirt and took a swig. The others eyed him with shades of bemusement, and he simply shrugged. "I don't know if it actually helps or not, but it doesn't hurt to play along." He offered water to the others, and it quickly made its rounds.

Then, they were off again, snaking through passageways and defying death in a dozen bizarre and exciting ways. Lord Celt seemed to especially enjoy the wall-jumping ascent they had to make to reach a "shortcut" the Sikh found, and CuddlyMoo-Moo all but giggled his way through the cave filled with fire-spewing mega-larvae.

It felt like another hour before they came to a hallway that could almost pass for normal, except for the row of skulls protruding from the wall at waist level for as far as they could see. The walls had a pale blue glow to them, although there was no obvious light source besides their green necklaces.

The Sikh paused for everyone to recover their strength. "Just ahead, you will find what you are looking for. Be very careful," he cautioned, one hand on his heart, the other aimed down the hall. "You may not recognize the man you find, and you may mistake him for helpless. Do not be fooled—stay back, and keep up your guard. You cannot overestimate what he is capable of."

The dwarf plodded forward, gazed down the

hallway, and aimed his axe in the same direction as the Sikh. "You expect us to just walk on down there without you? How do we know this isn't a trap?"

The Sikh exhaled sharply through his nose, his eyes shifting from one person to another. "Why would I bring you this far if I meant to harm you? I could have killed you a hundred times along the way here."

Lord Starr walked over to CuddlyMooMoo's side and cocked his head. "So, what, you're just going to stay here? Or go back? We're doing this as much for you as for us...unless you have some other agenda."

The Sikh sighed and tucked his hands in his sleeves. "I desire to end this dilemma. However, I also wish to not appear as a traitor to my clan leader. So perhaps you can forgive my reluctance to accompany you on the final leg of this journey."

Zero and Celt joined the others. "Thank you for your guidance," Lord Celt said. "We can finish the job from here." He ushered the other Lordz toward what they all hoped was the answer to their shared nightmare.

As they made their way down the corridor, the blue glow grew brighter. The hallway curved off to the right, so they had no way of telling how far it went.

After a few minutes, they had lost sight of the Sikh, and the blue light still beckoned from afar, now almost as bright as a fluorescent lamp. A hundred yards later, they were shielding their eyes from the brilliance. The Lordz began to stagger along, dazzled by the glow and running into each other and the walls.

Lord Starr stumbled over a lip in the path but kept his balance. When he looked up, he saw he was in a huge cavity, perhaps a hundred feet across and twice as tall, made of jagged blue crystals. No, not crystals...ice.

"Careful!" he warned the others, his breath clouding the air. They picked their way into the middle of the room, where their eyes were drawn immediately upward. Shards of ice radiated from the walls, glittering, beautiful, and deadly.

"Who's there?" Everyone looked around for the rasping voice, but the echoes obscured the source. "What do you want?"

Lord Starr noticed him first. Protruding from ice, buried up to his shoulders, was Jake.

CHAPTER 34
REVELATIONS

Lord Starr had to fight the instinctive urge to help Jake out of the ice. Starr crouched down to better face him. Up close, he noticed Jake's eyes were completely white—no iris, no pupil. Down in the ice, he could make out the source of the intense light: a glowing amulet hanging down from Jake's neck.

"Jake..."

Jake coughed. "What's going on? Do I know you? Can you get me out of here?" His blue lips trembled, and frozen tears formed a trail down each cheek.

CuddlyMooMoo strode forth, gripping his axe. "Sure—I can get some of you out of there in no time!"

"No!" Lord Starr's voice rang throughout the space. He stood, a hand raised protectively. "We promised we would hear him out first. And who knows what would happen to us all if we...it might make this all worse."

"What's he going to tell us?" the dwarf asked. "He's blind and trapped in ice! He doesn't know anything!"

Lord Starr turned to Zero, who had just floated Kit down onto the ice to take a breather. "Zero, is there anything you can do to help Jake out?"

The mage hung her head, hands in her robe sleeves. "I am drained, Lord Starr. He seems to be trapped in enchanted ice...I would need to be at full power to even make a dent."

Jake tried to turn his head toward Zero, but couldn't. "Who are you people? Am I gonna die?"

Lord Starr placed a tentative hand on Zero's shoulder. "Could you at least help him see?"

Zero sighed deeply, her eyes glowing yellow. "I'll try." She raised her arms, and the air rippled in front of them toward Jake's eyes. He recoiled slightly when the magic reached him, but then seemed entranced. The whitish film faded from his eyes, revealing dark brown irises beneath.

"Whoa, what the—!" Jake's mouth and eyes went wide. Suddenly, the ripples reversed and Zero crumpled to the ground.

"What did you do?" the dwarf shouted, raising his axe. He made for Jake again.

Jake winced. "I didn't do anything! I don't know what's going on!"

Three paces from striking Jake, CuddlyMooMoo

stumbled, his axe spinning across the ice toward the other end of the cave. He did not get up.

Lord Celt tensed up, gripping his sword hilt and flaring his nostrils, but remaining far from Jake. Lord Starr stood between his clanmate and the Bleaker, arms raised to keep the peace. "OK, OK...let's just take a second here." He looked back and forth at the two. "The Sikh told us it would be dangerous coming here, so let's not make it worse. Let's just talk, and we can see what's going on, all right?"

Celt pointed his sword at Jake, sneering. "We came here to end this nightmare, and he's behind it!" He gestured toward Zero, Kit, and the dwarf. "You don't fix this by *talking!*"

Jake's chin dropped, his face scrunching up. He sniffled. "I don't know what's happening. I swear, I didn't do anything to your friends. Look at me, I can't even move my arms!"

Starr held both hands toward Celt as if he were trying to open a very sensitive safe. "Please, let me try. If I drop...do what you gotta do."

Lord Celt clenched his jaw, his eyes smoldering. He snorted and looked away, releasing his sword.

Exhaling heavily, Lord Starr dropped his arms and turned back to Jake. He knelt nearby and raised his eyebrows. "Jake, do you know how you ended up like this?"

Jake looked up at him, then back down at the ice.

"It was during the attack on our fort...a couple clans teamed up against us and started ransacking the place. Typical stuff, for sure, and we were holding our own at the beginning. Nothing we haven't dealt with before."

He swallowed hard. "Then I heard The General was after me. That guy has had it out for me for months. Not that I wouldn't love to have his head on my trophy wall...but he came in ragin'—like, my guys *ran* when they heard him screaming and charging through walls of flame like a psycho. A bunch of them told me to get gone, said Sulla wouldn't stop 'til he got me. So I made for these tunnels."

"Get to the point, Smurf," Celt said, stretching his neck.

Jake writhed violently, growling. "You wanna trade places, Big Red? I've been stuck here for who knows how long, I can't talk to anyone—"

"We're all trapped here!" Lord Celt bellowed. "None of us can log out, we can't contact anyone except face to face, people are dropping left and right ever since you disappeared!"

Jake scowled. "So what, I'm behind it all? You think I did this to myself?"

"No...I did." Everyone looked around for the source of that voice, distant but familiar. Heavy footsteps approached from down a dark passageway at the far end of the chamber. When they hit the ice at the edge of the room, it cracked beneath them.

Lord Starr's heart climbed into his throat. He took a deep breath. "General Sulla."

CHAPTER 35
FIRE AND ICE

Sulla strolled across the icy floor, eyes fixed on Jake the whole time. "What Jake was trying to tell you was that he ran from me like the coward he is when I saw him in his rotten little town. He tried to lose me down some side streets, and just as he was going to dive down one of his rat holes, I—do you want to tell them, Jakey?"

The General stood a few feet away from Jake, crouching down like a kid who spotted a frog in the grass. Jake leaned away as far as he could, which wasn't much.

"C'mon, it's the best part of the story, Rippa my boy. No? You want me to tell it? Oh, all right." Sulla mussed Jake's hair playfully, except not really playfully at all.

Sulla stood again and circled the protruding head. "I swung my Slaked Sword, launching an energy blast straight at you. You hopped down that tunnel, certain you had avoided my attack. Except you didn't—it was delayed-release, stuck right to your back. Ten seconds later, it went off with that blue flash we've all been so worked up about."

The General looked up at the others as if noticing them for the first time. "It would have been perfect, too—Jake was supposed to be frozen in place, trapped in a duplicate world I made on another server. He wouldn't have been able to log out or respawn until I got around to ending him."

Lord Starr shook his head. "But your Slaked Sword shoots fire and lightning—I used it myself."

Sulla smirked and reached behind his head. "You used one of them—The Flame Edge. Meet...the Frostbrand." The General drew free a long, narrow weapon, clearish blue, like a huge jagged icicle. He eyed its length with sickening awe. "This...this was crafted with one purpose: to end the tormenting by this soulless executioner and give us all the freedom to enjoy this place as it was meant to be: a safe haven from the monsters of the world."

He whirled around to Jake again. "But you had to go and ruin that, too, didn't you?" He kicked Jake in the face. The back of his head rebounded off the ice, and his eye almost immediately began to swell shut. The General sucked in his breath. "Ooh, that looks really bad...do you want me to get some ice for that?" He guffawed, but when no one else joined him, he turned on them with a baleful glare. "Not in the mood for a laugh, Lordlings?"

Lord Celt drew his sword and marched toward Sulla. "This ends now!" He took two more steps, then, just like that, Lord Celt pitched forward, sprawling limply on the ice.

Sulla looked down at the fallen Lord and smirked. "Impressive prediction."

Lord Starr's stomach churned, an awful sourness filling his mouth. "Who are you? What is the point of all this? You made this game a prison for us. You're hurting real people in real life—my friend is in a coma, Kit is...I don't know, in some kind of limbo... How? Why?"

The General stalked forward, squinting at Lord Starr with confusion and disgust. "Are you seriously feeling sorry for this—this murderer? He terrorizes people, everything he has, he stole...he killed your chubby little sidekick! And he tried to execute me..."

He walked behind Jake, twirling his ice sword. "Remember that, Jake the Snake? You stormed my town, stole our best loot, collected lots of heads...then you came for mine. You charged at me, then cut to the right, got behind me, and raised up that nasty little sword of yours..." The General raised the Frostbrand high, its glistening point aimed down at Jake's head. "And then you struck!"

With that, Sulla stabbed Jake, right where his neck

meets his left shoulder. The sword sank in all the way to the crossguard. Jake unleashed an ear-splitting scream, his face contorting as he writhed furiously in place. He screamed and screamed and screamed, sobbing and twisting in vain with animal intensity.

They had all seen dozens of people killed in this game before—had killed many themselves, up close. This was nothing like that. This was viscerally gruesome, unwatchable, grotesque. Lord Starr didn't think Jake's screams could get any louder, only to realize he was also screaming.

The General just watched Jake with sadistic pleasure. "Don't worry, Jakey boy...I missed your heart, so you won't die on me. The ice will keep you from bleeding out. You'll just get to feel this pain until someone unplugs you, which I have a feeling won't be for a long time."

Lord Starr drew his sword but stayed back. "If you did all this to kill Jake, just kill him and end it! We shouldn't all have to suffer for your sick vendetta!"

The General glowered, his voice low and gravelly. "Suffer? What do you know about suffering? When you leave this game, you have a nice, normal life, don't you? You can go outside, you can talk with your friends, you can eat with your family...I used to do those things, a lifetime ago..."

Sulla's weapon drooped at his side as he looked up at the crystalline ceiling. "I've been locked in for two years now. At least, I think that's how long it's been...I was just riding my bike, when a car came out of nowhere, onto the sidewalk. I woke up in the hospital. Couldn't move anything below my eyelids.

"I don't know how, but one of the nurses realized I was still aware, inside. I could blink at her, and we worked out a language of sorts. I got the name of the drunk driver who hit me. Found out he got off with a few months and some community service.

"Anyway, I managed to get hooked up with the Interface early on...they tested it on people with my condition to see if it truly responded to brain activity only. I figured what's the harm? I didn't have much else to lose."

A wistfulness took over his expression, and his whole body lightened. "I was alive again, here. I could talk, I could run, I could be a person for the first time in..." His shoulders sagged ever so slightly, his eyes drifting toward Jake, who now just sobbed and shook. "And then I heard this guy was some kind of big deal in-game. I asked around about him, and he must've heard about me. That's when it got bad..."

Gritting his teeth, Jake managed to pull himself together enough to aim his wobbly head toward Sulla and sneer. "Seriously, dude? It's just a *game*! Part of the point is to attack people and get cool stuff. You're gonna make me a villain over that? That's why people play!"

Sulla slammed his fist into the ice by Jake's shoulder, kneeling with his face by Jake's ear. "You tortured me every day. You found out I was hooked up permanently to the Interface, so I never had a safe period. You told me you were just waiting for me to go to sleep so you could kill me. 'Don't go to sleep, Sulla...I'll carve you up tonight!' You made my life Hell!" The tears that fell and froze on the ground were now The General's.

Lord Starr looked toward Kit and Zero and Celt, all lifeless on the ground. There was a lump in his throat as big as a fist. His sword rattled in his hand as he stepped toward the two rivals.

"I came all this way to save my friends. If someone needs to die for that to happen, I will make it so. And if I need to end both of you just to be sure, make no mistake, that will happen. I am not going to let you—"

"Me. Kill me." Without looking up, Sulla drew his Flame Edge and offered it, hilt first. "I'm nearly gone, as it is. My family is pulling the plug on me in a few hours. I'd rather go on my terms if I can."

Lord Starr took the Slaked Sword. He felt the incredible power vibrating through his arms. It almost lifted itself to strike The General down. Holding the blade above his head, Lord Starr closed his eyes.

"Wait!" Jake grunted and winced as he turned his

head. He squinted at Lord Starr as he slowly lowered the blazing brand. "Killing him won't end this...everyone will still be trapped...as long as this amulet is protecting me..." He looked down at the glowing light beneath the ice.

Sulla, still staring at the ice, snorted out a puff of mist. "It's Shiva's Warding Amulet—one of a kind, forged from the tears of the goddess herself. You can't kill him unless he takes it off."

Lord Starr's head echoed with a dozen voices, each one telling him to do something different. *Kill them both! Run away! It's just a game—get out while you can! This is too big for you to fix, find someone who knows what to do!*

"Everett! Everett, honey, what are you doing!"

"Don't touch him, Janet—you saw what happens to kids when they get unplugged!"

"Well, we have to do something! Everett, can you hear us?"

"Mom? Dad?" Lord Starr looked around for their faces but saw only ice, pulsing light, the fallen and the soon-to-be-dead. "I don't know what to do!"

"Everett, sweetie, we're right here! Tell us what's going on—what should we do?"

He took a deep breath, seeing now his room, his parents in front of him, overlaid on the ice cave, like when a movie dissolves from one scene to another. "I'm trapped in a separate—it doesn't matter right now. I have two guys in front of me involved in this whole mess, and they're both telling me I need to kill one of them...I don't know...I'm scared..."

He heard his mom start to sob, and his dad comforting her. Then Dad cleared his throat. "They said on the news they were trying to find the guy responsible for the hack—as soon as his account is deactivated, they think it will break the spell, in a manner of speaking."

"So I'd have to execute him..." Everett looked at the blade in his hands, the blood and fire coursing below its surface almost compelling him to take a life, any life.

His dad's face faded in and out on the icy backdrop, visibly fighting to control the ache in his voice. "Um, if that's what you—yeah, in the game, I think that would do it."

Lord Starr closed his eyes and just tried to breathe normally. "OK. What's the worst that could happen?" He willed his muscles to stop shuddering, and he held the sword with both hands to steady it as he refocused on the game world.

Lord Starr couldn't make sense of the scene now before him. The General's sword no longer protruded from Jake's neck, and Jake's head no longer protruded from the ice; his head was now encased in ice, and the Frostbrand was gone. Gone with it was The General, his distant footsteps as soft as falling snow.

CHAPTER 36
BREAKAWAY

"Everett! What's going on? What should we do? Oh my god—"

Lord Starr sank the Flame Edge into the ice around Jake's body, carving a wide circle around it. "Mom, I need you to just hold on a minute...I'm gonna try something, and then I might have you pull me out."

"Like unplug you?" his Dad said. "I'm not going to risk putting you in a coma—"

"You have to trust me...I'm not like everyone else in this game." Holding the fire sword parallel to Jake's body, Lord Starr channeled the flaming energy downward. The ice began to soften, melt, and fracture, and water began to slosh up from the crevices.

Sweating and gritting his teeth, Lord Starr endured the blazing heat, coming closer to freeing Jake from this icy cell each second. When the ice began to fissure around Jake's chest and arms, Lord Starr dropped the sword and fell back, panting and half-blinded by the glowing blade.

Once he blinked most of the glare away, he lunged toward Jake's chest. He punched at the ice, grabbed fragmented corners, and raked at the edges to pull the wilting chunks of ice away. Wriggling his fingers into a breach, he pried until two plates of ice hinged away and fell. Lord Starr redoubled his efforts, gouging ice from Jake's arms, shoulders, and finally head.

When his head was free from the ice, Jake breathed fast and hard. "You could have started with my face, dude," he gasped.

Lord Starr sank back on his heels and wiped his brow. "Then I would have had to listen to you talk the whole time." He retrieved the Flame Edge from the icy ground beside him and examined it thoughtfully.

"So, are you gonna get me outta here, or go chase The General, or…?"

Lord Starr didn't answer, but instead peeled and chipped away more ice, so that soon Jake's entire upper body was free. His hair was dreadlocked with frost, but the purplish hue was fading from his skin.

"All right, now my legs…"

Lord Starr liberated Jake's sword from the sheath on his back before Jake could grab it. "Just a minute…we haven't discussed a game plan yet."

Jake rolled his eyes and heaved a sigh. "What?"

"You, me, most of our friends, we're all stuck in this game. The General put us here. If we don't work with him to get us out, ice or no ice, you're stuck for good. And that's actually bad."

"So...what? You're gonna talk to him and he's gonna hack my head off or whatever to get back at me? Is that what this is about?"

"I don't know what he's going to do. But I know you're the reason he did this, so you can be the reason it ends."

"I didn't do anything! This is a *game*, dude! What, we're all supposed to be nice to each other and just collect weapons for fun? It's a conquest kind of game! If you don't like it, don't play!"

"Yeah, except it's not just a game now. And for Sulla, it seems like it never was. It's his life. And now it's all of ours, too." Lord Starr took a knee, his hands upturned. "Look, if this is just a game to you, who cares what Sulla wants? If you work with me, I can get you out. If you don't, Sulla's gonna find you. Either way, you're dealing with the guy...wouldn't you rather have it on your terms?"

Jake just looked away, clenching his jaw. Lord Starr stood back up and looked toward the far wall.

"Mom, Dad, can you hear me?"

"Yes, honey, we're still here. Is everything all right?"

"Yeah...I think I'm set to come out. Dad, can you

stand behind me and catch me when I fall?"

Lord Starr looked at the amulet around Jake's neck. He saw a dark outline, like a person's shadow, moving before his eyes, around to his back. "OK, bud, I'm ready."

"Thanks. Now, Mom, I'm gonna have you pull the cord out of my head, but wait until Dad catches me and my eyes open. Got that?"

"After you fall, wait for your eyes to open. Yes."

"Perfect. Give me another thirty seconds." Lord Starr turned his back to Jake and began to rifle through his inventory.

"What are you doing? Where are you going? I'm still stuck here, man!"

Lord Starr took two items from his supply and turned back toward Jake. "Don't worry, I'll be right back. In the meantime, you can think about my offer while you dig yourself out." He tossed a small, worn-down dagger on the ground near Jake's waist.

"Seriously? A busted dagger? This'll take me all day to chip my way out!"

"Then I guess you better get started." Lord Starr worked on prying a large, clear gem from a jeweled gauntlet. Once it popped free, he examined it in the light. Satisfied, he positioned the crystal in the air between his face and the pulsing amulet. A riot of colors flashed at his eyes.

"All right, Mom...I'm coming home."

CHAPTER 37
UNPLUGGED

"Why aren't his eyes opening? Where is he?" Everett's mom's hand trembled, poised to yank out the Interface cord.

His dad was sweating, his forearms bracing Everett's limp form under the armpits. "We have to trust him, hon. He said to wait—"

Everett shuddered and arched his back, then drooped. His breathing became slow and shallow.

"Mike, what's happening? Oh my God!"

"I don't know! Did you touch the cord?"

"No, I didn't—it's still in there!"

"Can you—call Karen and ask her what happened when she unplugged Alex!"

Everett's mom threw up her hands. "I'm not gonna ask her that! You wanna ask her why her husband left her?" She paced around the room with a palm on her forehead.

Everett's dad closed his eyes and took a deep breath. "All right, we need to stay calm." He lowered Everett carefully to the ground. "Is there anyone we know who has this Interface thing—besides next door—who can maybe talk us through what to do here?"

"Jeff Wenger."

Everett's parents both nearly got whiplash looking at Everett, whose eyes fluttered open. "We need to go to Jeff's house."

Everett's dad propped up his shoulders as his mom scrambled back to his side. She took a deep breath and pulled out the cord.

Everett sat the rest of the way up. "Thanks, Mom. Can I have some water?"

"Sure, honey." She stroked his hair, her eyes glistening. "You know how much trouble you're in right?"

Everett couldn't help but smile a little. "Yeah...can you wait until tomorrow to kill me?"

His mom tousled his hair, nodded, and went downstairs.

Everett's dad sat on the floor beside him. "So, what do you want to do at this Jeff kid's house?"

Everett wrapped his arms around his knees and examined his hands. "Actually, there's a few things I need to do first. I think I know who's behind this whole mess." He looked up at his dad. "I just need to research some car accidents."

Thirty minutes later, Everett was on the phone with the parents of a Frankie Sullivan in Secaucus, New Jersey.

"Is this some kinda prank? Frankie can't come to the phone—"

"No, ma'am, sorry, I'm not—I know Frankie. Sort of. I know he's—what did he call it? Locked in. And he told me that he didn't have a lot of time—"

Mr. Sullivan's face appeared next to his wife's on the screen of Everett's phone. "You think this is funny? Where are your parents, you little snot-nosed—"

"We're right here, sir." Mr. Starner leaned in-frame and gave a tight smile. "Honestly, I know this is hard to hear, but my son has good reason to believe he has been in contact with Frankie. He has been playing a game, *Realms of Glory*, which your son apparently has access to. Have you heard of the Interface?"

Mr. and Mrs. Sullivan exchanged pained looks. He drew her close, tucking her head under his chin. Her hand must've dropped because the phone screen went grayish for a moment.

Mr. Starner squeezed Everett's shoulder encouragingly, and his mom rubbed his back. When Everett's phone showed the Sullivan's faces again, there wasn't a dry eye amongst them.

Mr. Sullivan thumbed away a tear. "What did he tell you?"

It took a while, with a bit of glossing over the harsh parts, but Everett managed to explain Frankie's life as General Sulla, the clashes with Jake, and the recent problems with the Bleak Clan. He ended with the whole separate-server-gone-wrong situation.

Mrs. Sullivan wrung her hands. "We knew he was up to something. His nurses told us the—the Interface thing was helping with his therapy. When he started asking them—not really asking, he just blinks, but they understand—he asked for books about programming and—Bernie, you remember…?

"Yeah, they said he asked about setting up a server. Wanted to practice his coding. He just seemed so driven, so with it, in a way. We thought we had a Stephen Hawking on our hands." He gave a sad sort of laugh.

Mrs. Sullivan sighed ruefully. "Then he started to turn. He had that—that headset on all the time. He wouldn't communicate with the nurses, except 'put it back on'…his vitals got low, it was just…the Interface went from being a way to bring him out of this, to something that seemed to ease him down the other way." Her voice caught and she turned away. "We are so sorry, we had no idea...we just had so much hope..."

Everett's mom sniffled and tried out a faint grin. "There still is hope, for our boys, and many others. We are so sorry to put you through all this, especially at this painful time, but our son truly believes he can fix this mess.

"The last thing we want to do is drag out anyone's suffering...but would you please consider holding off on—consider giving Frankie a little more time? I'm not asking you to decide this second, but could you please consider it? This is a lot bigger than any one of us."

The Sullivans huddled close, talking in low, sad, encouraging tones to each other. After searching each other's eyes and sniffling a good deal, they nodded. Mr. Sullivan kissed his wife on the forehead and then faced the phone screen again.

"No." He cleared his throat. "No, we don't need any more time to think this over. We will call the hospital and tell them to keep our boy here." His eyes shifted to Everett's, piercing them. "Please, save your friends. And if you can do anything for our Frankie..."

Everett struggled to swallow, his lips bunched together. "I will, sir. I'll do everything I can."

They ended the call soon after with an unexpected lightness in their hearts. Everett's parents rubbed his back. "We're proud of you, son."

Everett exhaled and smiled faintly. "Thanks for

being here." He tossed his phone on the bed and ran his hand through his hair. "Now for the hard part."

CHAPTER 38
SPECTACLE

"Uh, hey, Sta—Everett. Mr. and Mrs. Starner. Please, come on in." Jeff Wenger stepped back from the door, gesturing humbly. Everett tried not to savor Jeff's meekness too much, but he was only human.

They filed in and Jeff closed the door. Everett made for the basement, but his parents hung back and took the place in. Jeff's mother came into the main hallway from the kitchen, drying her hands on her apron.

"Well howdy, y'all! Can I get ya anything? Something to drink, maybe, to take the edge off? It's a real tongue-parcher today!"

Everett's mom smiled warmly and raised a hand. "Oh, no, thank you, we're fine."

"You have a beautiful home," Mr. Starner added. He rocked on his heels.

Mrs. Wenger fluttered her hands in the air.

"Where are my manners? Let me show you downstairs. Everyone else is already waiting on us!"

They trooped down the steps and entered the spacious gaming area. The boys were already gearing up, but there were some people in suits in the far corner, as well as a camera crew from the local news. Jeff went over the hookups for the custom Interface setup, as much for Everett's benefit as for the viewing audience.

"What Ev-Man sees in the game, we can see on this wall. That means your kids—their characters, anyway—will be up there, hopefully up and kicking goblins in the face before too long."

The reporter on scene, a chipper blonde with too much make-up, gave a fake laugh. She then aimed the mic at Everett. "All right, now—Everett, correct? We are going to watch you enter this alternate version of the game, where it seems that dozens, maybe hundreds, of players are trapped. How is it that you've been able to come and go?"

"Um, yeah, so..." Everett wasn't sure if he should look at the woman or the camera, so he split the difference. "I have photosensitive epilepsy, which means flashing lights can trigger a seizure. When I played *Realms of Glory* with a VR set-up—virtual reality headgear and sensors—I would sometimes black out from the blinking screen.

"Luckily, the Interface was developed—" He

gestured toward the suits in the corner, who dipped their heads and offered curt waves "—so I can experience the game without any lights actually flashing in my eyes. I do, however, still have seizures... I had one shortly after this whole locked-in incident, which must have broken whatever connection the game had in my brain.

"Now I can sort of trick my brain into seizing if I need to get out of the game. That's obviously not safe, so I don't plan on making that my standard log-off." He paused for a few laughs in the room. "Hopefully after this expedition, I will be able to log out normally, along with all my friends." He gave the double thumbs up but watched the carpet.

The reporter smiled and turned back to the camera. "Awesome, thanks for that, Everett. Now we have with us some representatives from DeepDelve Gaming, the developers of the Interface equipment." She began walking toward the suits in the corner, but they waved her off emphatically. "Actually, they are in the middle of something, so we might catch up with them later. I'm going to throw it back to you, Brian, and you can check back in once things get moving here."

After kicking it back to the studio, the reporter took out her earpiece and went over to the DeepDelve reps. "Did you guys need time to prepare a statement, or did one of you want to sort of say a few words when we go back on the air?"

The shortest of the four, a square-built guy with glasses, stepped forward. "We don't want to give the impression that we are here in any official capacity. While we certainly hope Everett is successful in this endeavor, DeepDelve does not directly endorse what is happening." He aimed an apologetic hand toward Everett and looked over the top of his glasses. "Not that we doubt you, young man, but if something were to go wrong, then we would expect to make a statement disavowing any connection to this... undertaking."

Everett really wished Kit was there to explain what half of that meant, but he read the tone of the guy clearly enough to develop a thick layer of dread in his stomach. Outwardly, he raised his eyebrows and offered a partial smile to the man, then turned back to Jeff and his family to get his head in the game.

"OK, here's the plan," Everett said, donning the headset. "When I log in, I should be back at the ice cave where I left Jake. He's the guy that Sulla—Frankie—is out to get. I'm going to use Jake as bait, so Sulla will hopefully work with me to fix everything. Odds are, Jake will have to die—just in the game, don't worry, but it'll look and sound pretty gruesome." He took a deep breath and exhaled some of his anxiety.

"Then, we get everyone back on the old server,

and people should be able to log out like usual. For everyone in a coma, I'll give the signal for their families to unplug them. That should get them back to normal. But like I said, it depends on Sulla, so wait for my signal before doing anything out here, OK?" His parents and Jeff nodded, as did the reporter. The suits exchanged looks of doubt and whispered amongst themselves.

With that vote of confidence, Everett turned on the golden headset and took a seat. His eyes vibrated side to side, then his eyelids drooped. Everyone else's eyes turned to the screen on the wall.

CHAPTER 39
THE BOY WITH A THOUSAND EYES

A ceiling full of giant icicles glared down at Lord Starr, still radiating and reflecting a blue glow. An intermittent hacking reverberated around the chamber. Sitting himself up, he looked around and gathered the items he dropped. A few feet away, Jake stared at him, a storm gathering on his brow.

"Back so soon? Gee, I only lost feeling in my hands like two hours ago." Hack. Hack. Hack.

Lord Starr pulled himself to his feet with the help of the Flame Blade. "Look at you! You're almost down to your knees already." He swayed the sword loosely, like a pendulum, as he looked down at the blue-skinned Bleaker. "So, did you think about my offer?"

"You mean the deal where, either way, Sulla chops my head off? Yeah, it crossed my mind a few times. Very tempting." He threw the dagger to the side.

"Listen, as long as you have that amulet, you're safe." Lord Starr gestured toward the ice. "Relatively safe. You decide what happens to you. I'm just asking you to consider these people around you, too." He gave the viewing audience a slow sweep of the bodies on the cave floor: Kit, Zero, Lord Celt, and Cuddly-MooMoo. Their families might not recognize their avatars, but he hoped people understood that it could be their kids lying on that ice there.

Jake rolled his neck a full circuit, then held out his arms. "Fine. Deal. Now get me out of here so I can die without frostbite on my—"

"Uh, just so you know, a bunch of people are watching me play right now, so you might want to be careful what you say." Lord Starr fired up Sulla's sword and began carving through the remaining ice around Jake.

"What do you mean people are watching you play? You're using the Interface, right?"

Lord Starr stopped his arc at a semicircle and sighed. "I know a guy who has this pretty sweet set-up—his dad is very techy, and so what I see in-game, projects on his wall."

"So him and his buddies are getting their jollies off watching me freeze to death in this ice hole?"

"Well, him, and our parents. And some people who work for DeepDelve." He resumed his carving. "And a small news crew."

Jake's head nearly corkscrewed around. "A news crew? Like, people are watching this on TV?"

"A small news crew...but, yeah. Lots of people have kids trapped in here, and they want to see if we can get them out." He completed his path around Jake and began prying at the ice with the blade.

"Great. No pressure. So if I don't make The General happy, all the moms and dads out there can hate me on a more personal level."

Lord Starr propped a foot on the crossguard of the sword, smiled down at Jake, and rolled a hand in the air. "Or they could love you for making it all work out perfectly..." He really held the smile, trying to impress upon Jake that all those moms and dads were watching them through Lord Starr's eyes.

Jake seemed to have gotten the message. "Right, yeah, I mean, this is a good plan. We got this." Lord Starr leaned into the sword and a large crack zigzagged through the ice around Jake's legs. In about a minute, the two succeeded in releasing Jake from his icy shackles.

Jake flopped on his back, panting and laughing deliriously. Lord Starr puffed clouds of mist as he sat on the other side of the ice hole, worried that this might be his last taste of success today.

Sitting up and taking in the room as if for the first time, Jake began to smile. "So, Lord Starr...what are we gonna do with all your friends here? I mean, I'd love to help carry them out of here, but, ya know... sore neck."

Shrugging off the comment, Lord Starr rose. "They'll have to stay here for now. If they need to be close to Sulla to get revived, we'll deal with that later." He walked over and extended a hand. "For now, we just need to get you topside and talking with our...disgruntled mutual friend."

Jake leaned back on his hands, cocking his head to one side. "I thought you said Sulla would find me, sooner or later. Why don't we just sit tight here and let him come to us? Oh, that's right...because his folks are gonna yank his cord and the little Sully-Boy will go bye-bye. Hmm, guess time isn't really on your side here..."

A deep reservoir of rage began pumping its boiling fluid throughout Lord Starr's torso, vining down his arms and up his neck. If the people at home could truly see what he was seeing, this entire world just turned red. The Flame Edge flared up, white-hot, in his clenched fist.

"Oooh, struck a nerve there, didn't I? Whatcha gonna do, Starr-pants? Slash me up? Too bad that won't work...I gotta say, I'm pretty glad I ganked this amulet from your junk clan's warehouse. You guys weren't good enough to have half the stuff in there anyway. Guess that's why you don't anymore."

Lord Starr forced himself to swallow his bile and

breathe. He fought the tension in his back, his arms, his face. When he spoke, he strained to sound calm. "You'll want to come with me. Trust me."

Jake angled a hand over his mouth and blew a raspberry. "Try and make me. Your track record with wrangling the big dogs is pretty sus, though. I mean, The General was at your feet and he got away. You're outta your league."

Jake started for the tunnel Lord Starr originally entered from, and Lord Starr took a step to follow him. Jake snatched up the dagger he dropped early and held it forward, hunched over. "Ah-ah-aaah... Methinks you're a little too slow for that play, Star Child." He tugged on the chain of his amulet. "Can't touch this. Now run along. Have fun ticking off Sulla."

As Jake began to scurry off, Lord Starr put the Flame Edge tip-down in the ice and tilted his chin up. "Jacob Steven Kettering."

Jake paused. Turned.

"Sulla said you knew he was in the hospital. He didn't mention why." Lord Starr tipped his head slightly. Jake fidgeted with the dagger. "It's because you're in there, too."

Lord Starr twirled the sword in the ice idly. "When I talked to his parents, they told us all about you. They thought you two were best friends, sharing a room and all. Doing this Interface experiment together.

"That's why you're still running around, while

everyone else is...And he made sure no one would unplug you so you'd be stuck in here just like he planned."

Jake gave him a slow clap. "Great work, Sherlock. Now you'll make sergeant for sure." He saluted with his knife. "Sounds like I have all the time in the world to run."

"Not if I have a say in it." Lord Starr began to pace a slow circle. "I give the word, and the doctors will unplug your Interface like that." He snapped. "Kinda hard to run when you're comatose." Lord Starr looked at his fallen friends to drive the point home.

Jake shrugged. "You can't and you won't."

"Try me." Lord Starr crossed his arms and leaned casually on an icy stalagmite. "Would the doctors at Kent General get ready to pull Jacob Kettering's Interface cord on my command?"

Jake backed away, incredulous. "You really expect me to believe a bunch of people are watching this? Amateur bluff, son."

"One."

"What am I, a toddler? Peace out, girl scout." Jake turned to leave.

"Two."

"What, you're gonna put me in a *coma*? Are you insane?"

"Three. Doctor Robinson, please pull the—"

"Whoa!" Jake dropped the dagger and raised his

hands. "All right, OK, I'll go!" He looked around, his hands protecting the back of his head.

"Doctor Robinson, please stand down." Lord Starr raised an eyebrow expectantly.

Jake came over, dragging his feet. As he passed Lord Starr, he scowled. "Fascist."

"Oh, that reminds me...I'll take that amulet now."

Jake stopped, but he didn't reach for the talisman. "If you think for one second I will go with you to face Sulla without this amulet—"

Lord Starr merely held up one hand, his fingers poised to snap. Jake ripped off the amulet and threw it at his feet, then stormed off toward the tunnel Sulla took.

Stooping to pick up the talisman, Lord Starr took a beat to calm his roiling innards and bring his heart rate lower than the national debt. He then stood, fastened the amulet on himself, and marched after Jake, hopefully toward Sulla.

CHAPTER 40
SYMPATHY FOR THE GENERAL

The remains of the Bleaker's town smoldered all around them. Although it was late morning in-game, the sky was so thick with smoke that it might as well have been dusk. Lord Starr ushered Jake along more or less at sword-point, both picking their way over the hot and treacherous rubble. Smoke stung their lungs and eyes, and carried the scent of burnt flesh.

Through a gray haze, they saw a dark form on top of a mound of debris. As they drew closer, they could make out the silhouette of The General, broad, jagged, but stooped and motionless.

Jake came to a halt, resisting Lord Starr's prodding. "I'm not going up to him first...he'll take my head before I can say three words."

Lord Starr lowered the sword and took Jake by the arm. "It's just a game, right? What do you have to worry about?" He walked ahead, pulling Jake behind.

The wall of smoke became several thin veils, and then tendrils in a vague mist, so that Sulla's bulk took on detail. He was seated on the piled remains of a column, staring down at the ground. All around him, bodies lay contorted, slumped, dismembered, their clan markings rendered indistinguishable by blood and ash and ruin. They were all the same clan now.

Lord Starr walked wide around The General and the bodies, leading Jake to a spot walled in by rubble except for the side facing Sulla. He gave Jake a "stay put" look. Jake rolled his eyes and nodded.

Sheathing the Flame Edge as best he could, Lord Starr approached Sulla from his left side, stones crunching beneath each deliberate step. At least he hoped they were stones.

"What's it like?" The General's soft, vulnerable tone caused Lord Starr to stop in his tracks. "To leave this place and enjoy the real world? Is it as marvelous as I remember?"

Lord Starr found the least precarious stack of bricks and stone he could, sat upon it, and sighed. "Uh, well, I guess it's pretty good out there. Most people still complain about it now and then, but if I had to choose...I mean, I'm trying to get everyone out for a reason."

Sulla looked over, rolling a fragment of brick between his fingers. "I came here as an escape, to get away from all the pain and helplessness and..." He groaned. "And it all just followed me here. People are no different here than out there. Selfish, stupid, thoughtless, tearing everyone else down, ruining what others spent so long creating." The fragment crumbled to dust in his hand. "Either this place brings out the worst in people, or people are just jerks no matter where they are."

Lord Starr leaned forward and propped his chin on his fist thoughtfully. "Yeah, maybe. I mean, I come here to take my mind away from the bullies and the drama of real life, like a lot of people. And obviously it's not all peaches and glitter here, either..." His eyes swept the area: rubble everywhere, smoke still swirling, bodies as dead as ever, Jake as tense as a cornered badger.

Lord Starr put his hands on his knees and rocked to his feet. "But some great things happen here, too. A lot of us try to do the right thing, at least most of the time. We show some loyalty to our clans, to the people we care about."

Sulla dusted his hands. "Well, nobody cares about me."

"Are you kidding? You're The General! Half the guys in this game want to be you, and the other half are too busy being jealous."

"Yeah, jealous of this!" He flicked his hands down and outward to indicate his appearance. "This isn't the real me! This is who I want to be because I'm some pathetic, bedridden vegetable in a hospital somewhere."

He turned his gray eyes toward Lord Starr for the first time. "My own family doesn't even care about me. They sent me in here, and now they're going to pull the plug on me. Like I'm an appliance." He sniffled, but only once.

Clearing his throat, The General gestured toward the bodies in front of him. "But look what I did... maybe I deserve to end up like them. Obviously I do."

Lord Starr risked approaching Sulla, a calming hand outstretched. "But you can still do good, OK? You can make this right. You are a good person, Frankie. You're a good kid."

Sulla, slumped again on the rubble, looked down at his hands and shook his head. "No one deserves this, to be trapped in here..."

Lord Starr swallowed hard, standing now just a few steps from The General. "Can you bring us back?"

Sulla closed his eyes. "Maybe. Our other server still exists. The only reason we're stuck on this one is because I set it up to keep us all together until I killed Jake, leaving him and him alone in this hell."

"Right, so...if you execute Jake, we can all go back, correct? I already took the necklace off him, so we can do this—"

The General rose, now towering over Lord Starr. "Execute him? And let him off easy? No, I want him trapped here forever, alone, like I've been trapped in my body, and this place, all this time. Then I can die in peace."

"Well, you're not going to die until I say so. I talked to your family. No one pulls your plug until we get out."

Sulla broke off his glare at Jake and watched his own feet as he began to pace. "To break this loop keeping us here, Jake has to die."

Jake swaggered toward them, his arms out wide. "Then kill me—what do I care?" He stopped, his limbs dropping to his sides. "That's what I deserve. Your life is basically ruined out there, and it looks like I've ruined it in here. How could I face the world now?" He gestured toward Lord Starr's face. "They're all watching us through his eyes right now—your family, his family...probably not my family, but lots of people who have been stuck here because...because of me!"

His mouth and chin bunched up, and he tilted his head back to expose his neck. "So c'mon! Give me what I deserve! End me now!" His shrill voice echoed off the ruins of his former fortress.

General Sulla and Lord Starr stared at Jake's red face for a long moment, paralyzed by emotion. Sulla moved first, reaching his hand behind his head. "So be it." He unsheathed Frostbrand and launched a wave of ice at Jake, encasing him up the neck.

Jake and Lord Starr, equally shocked, stammered

an objection. Sulla silenced them with a hand, looking toward the crumbling ramparts in the other direction. "I'll get you out, but this is how it has to be done." He faced Lord Starr, aiming Frostbrand at him. "I will open the code to allow everyone back to the original server. Tell your fans back home—no, better yet…"

He got close to Lord Starr's face as if he were addressing a TV camera. "Hello? Yes, it's me, Sulla. Go plug your kids back into the Interface now. I'll give you a minute. Then when I say so, they will be able to log out normally. That should break the bad circuit in their heads, bring them back, and allow them to return to the game proper. Got that? Good."

He patted Lord Starr on the side of the face a few times, then pushed it away toward Jake. "While I do that, Lord Starr will have the honor of making you die."

Lord Starr's throat tightened. "What? Why me? You're the one who wants him dead!"

"And you're the one who wants to save all these nice people. If you want to clean up a mess, you have to get your hands a little dirty." Sulla pointed toward Lord Starr's back with Frostbrand. "Besides, you have my best sword already. It would be a shame to never get to properly use it."

Lord Starr's inertness drew Sulla and his menacing sword a few paces closer. "You do want your friends back, right? You don't want to let down all the people back in the real world that are counting on you, do you?"

Lord Starr exhaled, then reached for the Flame Edge slowly, his eyes burning with contempt.

"That's a good boy," Sulla mocked. "Make sure you take his head off in one blow...you know how people can sometimes come back from a bad execution attempt, right, Jakey?"

"You can't make me do this," Lord Starr said, not with defiance, but with a strange tenderness. "You'll become the kind of bully you despise. You don't want to end things like this." He lowered the sword. "Let's just get everyone home, OK?"

Sulla stared deep into his eyes, unblinking. "Everyone ready? Your kids can come home just as soon as Lord Starr lets Jake have it. Help him make the right choice." Sulla's eyes had an otherworldly intensity, a manic fervor. He was here, but he was not really here.

A wall inside of Lord Starr crumbled. Then another. In his heart, in his stomach, everything collapsed. He squeezed his eyes shut hard. "Fine." He took a ragged breath. "Fine." Opening his eyes, he lifted the sword. "But this is on your conscience, Sulla. This is on you, Frankie."

Lord Starr marched over to Jake. Jake shook his head, his eyes bulging from their sockets, his mouth wide. Lord Starr heard nothing but his own heart pounding in his ears. The Flame Edge swung high as if propelling itself, slicing the air toward Jake's neck as effortlessly as light passes through a window.

The force of the swing spun Lord Starr around, sparing him the sight of Jake's head, the blood, the gore. Instead, his momentum brought him to a stop fully turned around, so that he could see The General instead.

This gave him the unique opportunity to witness Sulla's knees buckle, his eyes roll back in his head, as gravity pulled The General down by the shoulders.

CHAPTER 41
COLLAPSE

A dozen pairs of eyes stared at the screen on Jeff Wenger's wall as Lord Starr screamed through the surround sound system. They saw him lunge toward Sulla's fallen body, trying to shake the life back into it.

Everett's mom stifled a cry with her hand. The short, stocky DeepDelve representative clenched his eyes shut and pinched the bridge of his nose. The reporter shook her head, repeating "no" over and over again.

Sulla's twisted visage filled the wall, gray and still as a statue.

"Why?" Lord Starr howled. "Who unplugged him? Why?!"

Everett remained seated in the chair, outwardly unperturbed. His dad put his hands on his shoulder and spoke close to his ear. "We'll figure this out, buddy. Let me call Frankie's parents." Mr. Starner watched the screen to see if Lord Starr reacted at all, but the sobbing continued unabated.

The DeepDelve rep strode toward the reporter, waving his hands. "We need to shut this down now!" He pointed at the screen. "This was not authorized by us, our presence here is not a sign of consent!" He pushed a camera away. "Shut them off!"

The room filled with the mumblings, shouts, strained phone calls, and muted weeping of its various occupants. Jeff's mom tried to calm everyone with some refreshments but was roundly rebuffed. The other DeepDelve reps tried to calm their spokesman down, but that just seemed to stoke his fire. Everett's parents huddled in a corner, each plugging one ear as they tried to reach the Sullivans.

"It is not clear what has just happened," the reporter said to the camera, her mascara smeared beneath her eyes. Two crewmembers restrained the DeepDelve spokesman, out of frame, while he struggled to interrupt the broadcast. "The players trapped in this part of the game were supposed to be released by General Sulla on the condition that Lord Starr—Everett here—executed Jake in the game."

The cameraman panned over to Everett, still slumped in the chair. The camera then went to the screen on the wall as the reporter gestured toward it. "The General has apparently been unplugged from the game—or maybe in real life, it's unclear—so the fate of the players still in this part of the game is very uncertain. The General was the only one who knew how to get them out."

Meanwhile, Mr. Starner got through to the Sullivans. Mrs. Sullivan was hysterical, and her husband could barely hold the phone still. "We don't know what happened—nobody touched his plugs... we're here with him, and one second he was doing everything you saw on screen, the next second..." The steady beep of a flatline droned in the background. "He's gone."

Everett's dad blanched. "We are so sorry, for your loss, for...for everything," Mr. Starner managed to say. "Would you like us to say a few words on your behalf, or would you like to wait...?"

The Sullivans went out of frame on Mr. Starner's phone, and their weeping blocked out all other sound. Mr. Starner and his ex-wife exchanged pained looks.

A deep rumbling shook the basement, sending everyone there into a defensive hunch. Lord Starr shouted. They all looked toward the shaking screen.

"What's going on? Oh my God, get me out of here!" On the screen, everyone could see the wreckage of Bleak Island shuddering and tumbling over. Cracks began to zigzag across the ground. The sky itself began to fissure.

The entire world was falling apart.

"Mom! Dad! Help!" Lord Starr dropped Sulla's

body and whirled around, directionless.

Everyone in the basement began talking over each other, exhorting someone to either unplug Everett or by all means don't touch his cord.

"ENOUGH!" The DeepDelve spokesman held up his hands in the center of the room. The basement fell silent, except for Lord Starr's panicked pleas. "The server is deleting everything because its host is gone. Without The General, the place cannot exist. Everyone in there will be erased in a few minutes, with no hope of retrieval."

He turned to the reporter. "I'm ready to make our statement now."

Mr. Starner surged forward. "So you're just gonna wash your hands of this and walk away? My kid is in there! He's trapped because your people don't even know how to make their own equipment work correctly! He's trying to save your sorry—"

"Sir, your son elected to take this risk. He made every assurance he could extricate himself from this virtual world. We made no promises that he would succeed. I'm sorry, but we didn't create this particular mess. Our system was compromised, voiding any culpability on our part—"

"Stop the legalese and just talk like a human for a minute!" Mr. Starner was a foot from the man's face, the picture of rage and fear and fatherly protectiveness all in one. "There has to be a way to—I don't know, access the code, stop this process—buy him time to get out of there!"

"Like I said, this is a closed system. Unless the player who initiated this sequence can end it, there's no way to stop anything."

"Send me in." A dozen heads turned toward the other side of the room. Jeff Wenger stood by his mom, his hands fidgeting at his side. "I can log in as The General. Let me go in and stop it."

His mother clutched at his arm. "Jeffrey, no! I won't have you go in there when everything is falling apart."

He held his free arm toward Everett. "And you're just going to let him die here in our basement?" Jeff turned to the DeepDelve spokesman. "Get me The General's log-in. Your all-star tech team can manage that, can't they?"

CHAPTER 42
FREEZE TAG

Lord Starr huddled over The General, not sure if he was trying to protect him or crush him. The rupturing ground sent shockwaves up his legs, and the sky thundered like an artillery bombardment. He squeezed his eyes shut and prayed for a way out.

"Dude...get off me."

Lord Starr's eyes snapped open to see The General stirring just beneath him. He rocked back to his feet, his hands grabbing at Sulla as if expecting him to vanish into smoke.

Sulla swept his hands away and sat up. "It's me, Jeff. I'm here to get you guys out."

Just as Lord Starr formulated his first coherent sentence, his thoughts were jarred by a second realization: the shaking had stopped. He looked around and saw that the sky, half torn asunder by raging lightning, was frozen mid-tear, silent. The ground now stood firm, the fissures here and there getting no wider or narrower. The edges of the island, curling toward them like tsunami waves, hung in the air, like a flower closing its petals for the night.

Lord Starr faced General Jeff. "How did you—how do we get out of here now?"

The General's arms rested on his bent knees, his mouth shifted to one side. "Um, I don't know exactly. I just know that *me*—" he did air-quotes "—being here would buy you guys some time."

"Can you log out?"

The General's eyes rolled from left to right. "Uh, yeah, it looks like it." He stood up and tried to dry his palms, only to discover he was completely covered in armor. "Wow, this guy is *savage*."

He shook off his awe and refocused. "OK, I talked with my dad before I came in here, and he said I should be able to complete the circuit—finish what Sulla started and get everyone out—by manually releasing each player. He said The General could probably do it all automatically, but without access to whatever he used, this will have to do."

"So...like freeze tag?"

General Jeff shrugged. "Worth a try." He pointed toward a body near Lord Starr's foot. "Who's that?"

Lord Starr leaned close and stood back up. "A Bleaker. RamboRecker213."

The General looked right in Lord Starr's eyes and

smiled. "RamboRecker213...get ready to log out." He touched the body, and a blue light radiated from his hand across its back, head, and limbs. Then nothing.

Lord Starr's lungs tightened, his eyes shifting between the body and The General. "What did that do? What did you do?"

"I don't know—my dad said it would work immediately, so we should see something—"

Just then, RamboRecker213 twitched. His hands moved up to his sides, pressing him away from the ground. He looked around with more than enough shock on his face to cover the desolation of his town, the dead all around, and the two guys standing over him that seemed super casual about the whole situation.

"What in the world is going on...?"

"Rambo, buddy, can you log out?"

The Bleaker unsteadily transferred from his knees to his feet. His eyes rolled back. "Yeah, yeah, I can."

General Jeff put a hand on his shoulder. "You should probably do that. Like right now."

RamboRecker213 swallowed, his gaze shifting from Lord Starr to The General. "Riiiight..." A second later, he blinked away, as if he had never been there.

Lord Starr shook his head and smiled at The General. "All right, let's get these guys home!"

The General went on to tag more of the players in

the immediate vicinity. Some did not respond, which he assumed meant that they were no longer plugged in. Others popped right up, apparently plugged in the entire time. He wasn't sure which scenario concerned him more.

Meanwhile, Lord Starr searched the wider area for more fallen. In his zeal to find each new body, he almost overshot a lone player lying face down by the ruins of the armory.

Wolfgang.

Lord Starr walked over to his fallen friend, placing a hand on his lifeless back. "Alex…" he whispered, his voice caught in his throat. "Jeff…JEFF!"

He began dragging Wolfgang back to the center of town when The General's footsteps came thumping closer. "Everett? Where are you?"

"Over here! I found Alex!" He laid Wolfgang's body down on a relatively flat area and knelt beside him as General Jeff trotted over.

The General examined the body, the grievous wounds, his twisted limbs and face. His heart sank. He turned to Lord Starr. "Did he feel it? Will he feel it?"

Lord Starr just stared down at his friend, faintly shaking his head. "I don't know." He looked up. "But we gotta get him out. Do you know if his mom hooked him back up to the Interface?"

The corner of The General's mouth drooped. "I'm not sure. I can log out quick and check, then jump back in...?"

Lord Starr took a deep breath and blew it out. "I don't want to mess this up. If you tag him and he's not hooked up, he might never come back." General Jeff neither confirmed nor denied the statement, himself unsure. "OK, log out quick and ask my parents. *Then come right back.*"

The General stood. "Of course...where else would I rather be?" He closed his eyes, hummed a moment, then went silent. He toppled sideways, hitting a partial wall with his shoulder on the way to landing face down in some smoldering debris.

Lord Starr winced, reaching to at least drag him away from the burning embers. No sooner did he grab The General's ankles and tug, though, than he was shaken off his feet.

The ground began to vibrate, then shift, then rumble. The edges of the island shook and rose, continuing now to curl in toward its center. The sky slowly resumed its crescendo toward thundering Armageddon.

A fissure formed down the very street they were on, snaking between Lord Starr and the fallen men. He lunged for Wolfgang and pulled him over, just as the crack widened. Lord Starr then reached for The General, whose legs now dangled into the growing crevice.

Just as he grasped for a hand, The General's arms

flew up, his eyes wide open. "He's plugged in!" he exclaimed, just as the chasm swallowed him whole.

CHAPTER 43
NO DWARF LEFT BEHIND

Lord Starr dove toward the chasm, watching The General's body pinball into the darkness below. His brain exploded into hyperdrive, all his fear and anger and despair churning in his mind. He didn't know which would burst first, his pounding heart or aching lungs.

He stayed there for a moment, certain there would not be another moment to follow this one, when he paused. Held his breath. The ground wasn't shaking anymore. The sky fell quiet again. The island's edges, perilously curved overhead, hung motionless as the moon. The collapse had stopped.

Lord Starr aimed his face at the crevasse. "Jeff! JEFF! Can you hear me? Say something!"

A distant groan made its way up. "That...hurt."

Lord Starr didn't care how many people were watching him just then—he jumped up, clapped his hands, and did a giddy dance. Then he remembered Wolfgang still lying on the ground. "Jeff, can you get back up?"

A delay, then: "Uh, maybe...but I think you'd rather come down. There's a tall ginger, a passed-out wizard, a cat babe, and some kind of disco-midget-biker down here that you'd probably like to see..."

Ten minutes later, Lord Starr came rushing into the ice cave, Wolfgang slung over his shoulder, and slid to a stop near Lord Celt, Kit, Zero, and Cuddly-MooMoo. He dumped Wolfgang on the ice, struggling to catch his breath. "Ok...tag Alex...then we can...get these guys out."

General Jeff twirled one hand theatrically and touched Wolfgang on the shoulder. The blue light special swept over his body, and a moment later, he was among the living again.

When he opened his eyes, The General and Lord Starr were smiling down on him like two old ladies looking at a newborn. "AHHHH!" Wolfgang shouted, grasping for his spear, which was nowhere to be found.

He sat up hurriedly, and the others stepped back to give him room, still smiling like idiots. "What are you guys doing? Where am I?" He looked around. "What happened to Kit and Zero? And who's the bearded beach ball?"

Lord Starr extended a hand and helped him to his

feet. "Dude...another time. First, we gotta get you outta here." Lord Starr gripped the sides of Wolfgang's arms and shook him. "Can you log out?"

Wolfgang's eyes darted around. "Um, yeah...this is just a game, right?"

Lord Starr pursed his lips and nodded. "Yep, just a game." He tousled Wolfgang's mangy hair, much to his annoyance. "Now seriously, get out of here. We can talk about all this on the other side."

"All right, all right..." Wolfgang twitched twice, then faded away.

Lord Starr didn't want to say anything out loud, but he was never happier to see his best friend disappear.

"OK, what about the rest of this circus?" General Jeff said with a sweep of his arm.

Lord Starr turned CuddlyMooMoo over with his foot. "Let's hope they're plugged back in by now. I'm not having you run out to double-check anymore."

The General tagged CuddlyMooMoo first. The dwarf rolled to his feet in a blink, his axe at the ready. "DIE, SULLA!" He charged the RoMAN, swinging his weapon so furiously he could barely keep his balance. General Jeff took off, screaming in fear.

Lord Starr tried to call him off between bursts of laughter. "Breaker! Breaker! Heel, boy! He's not really Sulla!" The enraged dwarf slowed and started sucking wind, allowing General Jeff to nurse the stitch in his side across the chamber.

Lord Starr jogged over to the dwarf, one arm aimed at The General. "A friend of mine took over Sulla's body because—ugh, can I just explain this to everyone once after we all get out of here?"

CuddlyMooMoo slowed his panting. "Get out of here? Whattaya mean get out—" He looked around. "Hey, I can log out now! I can log out!"

"I know, buddy, I know...go ahead. We'll catch up in a few."

CuddlyMooMoo holstered his axe and rubbed his hands together. "I can finally log out! I hope I didn't pee myself yet..." His arms went limp, and he faded away.

Next, The General tagged Zero, but nothing happened. He tagged her a few more times. No blue light. He looked to Starr.

Lord Starr's face was the picture of hope. "Keep trying...she's gotta be there."

General Jeff attempted a few more times, and suddenly the blue light spread over her robe. Her body lifted off the ground, and she stood herself upright without comment.

"Zero!" Lord Starr wanted to hug her but figured that would be too much. Instead, he held his arms forward while leaning back slightly. "Look at you! All floaty again! Yay!"

General Jeff just stood there, gazing at her face.

She pulled up her hood and looked at Lord Starr. "So...what's new?"

Lord Starr just laughed. "Good to have you back, Zero." He waved Jeff over. It took a few tries, but he finally pried his eyes off Zero and joined Lord Starr, who was kneeling next to Kit.

"Is the psycho witch your GF?" General Jeff whispered through clenched teeth. "Crazy, but *hot*..."

Lord Starr blushed. "No...she is." He propped Kit's head up on his lap.

"And you saved her for last?" Jeff shook his head. "Better not tell her that..." He tagged her shoulder. Once more, the blue light did its thing.

Kit's eyelids fluttered, her mouth trembled. She began to breathe, and when she opened her eyes, Lord Starr was the first face she saw, staring upside down at her with an eye-creasing smile.

"Everett," she whispered, her purple cat-eyes twinkling, "you saved me..."

General Jeff coughed. "For last..."

Kit propped herself up to see better. "Sulla? What are you doing here?" She looked around. "Where is *here*?" She spun around on her seat to face Lord Starr. "What's going on?"

Lord Starr took her hands and grinned. "I promise, I'll explain everything." He looked over Kit's shoulder toward Zero. "To both of you."

"Yeah, the important thing is that *I* saved the day,"

General Jeff bragged, holding his hands out to gather the showers of praise he expected. There were none in the forecast.

"Yeah you did," Kit said, but she was looking right at Lord Starr. She put her arms around his neck and gave him a gentle peck, which immediately replaced his accident with the Christmas lights as the most electrifying moment of his life.

Jeff, his hands still out, rolled his eyes toward Zero.

"Not in a million years, General." She hovered toward Kit. "Apparently we can log out now, so...let's do that."

Kit stepped back to arm's length from Lord Starr and smiled at the mage. "Yeah, good idea." She caressed Lord Starr's cheek. "See you on the other side..."

Lord Starr gave her a confused semi-smile. "Not if I...see you first?"

Despite the cheesiness of the line, Kit laughed and took Zero's hand. "OK, girl, let's bounce." The two fidgeted a little and then faded away.

Lord Starr, still riding high on endorphins, turned to General Jeff with a grin. He clapped the hulking man on the shoulder and began steering him toward the surface. "All right, just 200 more to go..."

CHAPTER 44
AFTERMATH

Mr. Wickenheiser drew a line through the array of points. "Now, notice how most of the data is clustered around the line, but we have this one outlier—"

The bell rang, triggering a chorus of chatter, closing books, and zipping backpacks. Mr. Wickenheiser waved his yardstick at the homework listed on the board and tried to shout over the ruckus, but gave up mid-sentence.

Everett slipped out of the room last, running into Alex in the hall. They did their usual fist-bump-handshake combo and then got down to business.

Alex tossed his hair out of his eyes. "ROG after school?"

"Uh, yeah, I should be able to. I have a lot of homework, but I'll do some on the bus." They passed a cluster of girls who giggled and waved. The boys waved back, but Everett avoided eye contact.

As they kept walking, Alex looked back and then

slapped Everett on the shoulder. "What's your problem? Those eighth graders were checking you out!"

"I *have* a girlfriend," Everett protested with a smile.

"You don't have to rub it in." Alex smirked as he elbowed Everett playfully.

They turned left at the end of the hall and made for the front doors. Jeff Wenger and his crew merged with the crowd from the other side. He bobbed his head to Everett from across the lobby.

"Ev-man!" He hustled over with one arm out, the universal sign for a bro-hug. They clasped hands and drew together for a chest bump.

Everett then greeted the rest of Jeff's squad, who gave a what's up to him and Alex. Everett pulled on his backpack strap. "You wanna ROG tonight?"

"If you're playing, I'm there!" Jeff exclaimed. His buddies seconded the motion.

"All right, I'll text you—" Everett started, but Jeff was already walking away, toward the rest of the lacrosse team. "I'll just text you then."

A few other kids said Everett's name in passing, and he took a minute to answer some *Realm of Glory* questions from a tenacious sixth grader. Everett knew he still wasn't Mr. Popular, but at least he was known for being good at *something*. That's a big social upgrade in his book.

He clambered up the bus steps a minute later, apologizing to the driver for holding her up again. He swung into his seat—the back left corner—and immediately took out his phone. He fired up Snapchat and grinned irrepressibly when he saw "KitKate" with a 120 and a flame next to it.

Her snap was a picture of her shoe with the label Sup?

He snapped back a blurry shot out his bus window and tagged it Cruisin'

They exchanged messages the rest of the ride, eventually building to four- and five-word phrases in a shot. Though they didn't write a lot, they said so much. They'd been through a lot together over the past four months, mostly little things: drama with friends, school stress, parent grief. Plus, he helped her overcome her fear of ever using the Interface again. They made a pact that neither one would go in without the other, and they both waited a good month for that, waiting to see if anything at all went squirrelly before diving back in.

Perhaps most important of all, though, she helped him make it through Frankie's funeral.

That was the first and only time they'd actually met, a two-hour drive for both of them, but from opposite directions. Even as his eyes welled up with tears, his heart wanted to burst with joy when he saw her. They barely said ten words to each other the entire time—what does anyone remember saying at a funeral anyway?—but just her being there made all the difference. Their moms talked for a good twenty minutes after the service, but they just sat together in the back of the funeral parlor, looking at their shiny black shoes and quietly holding hands.

As the bus slowed down to drop Everett off, he shot Kate a quick TTYL and slung his backpack on before rushing toward the exit. He hurried through the front door, to the kitchen counter, greeting his mom along the way. In no time, he had his homework spread out, half a snack devoured, and his phone at-the-ready on the stool next to him. He was especially proud of how convincingly he faked a conversation with his mom while she unloaded the dishwasher.

An hour later, he shoved his papers back in his binder—somehow managing to get 90% of his math right and most of his rough draft done for social studies—and headed for his room. "Mom, gonna play ROG for a little before dinner!"

She angled her head over the banister and called up the steps, "All right, but as soon as your dad gets here, you need to come down!"

"Got it!" He closed his door and kicked off his shoes. Even though he had his new Interface setup for two weeks now, he still got a thrill every time he saw it. It was the latest version, available only to Deep-Delve preferred stockholders, which he became shortly after "The Glorious Rescue."

This Interface, besides being 60% lighter and even more responsive, had two crucial features: one, it was wireless, eliminating the danger of accidental unplugging, and two, it hosted a mirror of the gaming world, so it was impossible to ever get stuck on another server again.

Moments later, Everett was lying back on his bed, and Lord Starr was gallivanting about Lordz Landing, overseeing the massive new expansion to the south. Kit was by his side as he set the NPCs' task queues, designed the new soaring double walls (everyone wanted to try raiding them now that LORDZ were top dogs in the Realm), and did a midday guard shift.

Just as the two of them had a minute of unstructured time, Wolfgang caught up with them just outside the newly christened "CuddlyMooMoo Petting ZooZoo". He seemed excited as he ran up, but not necessarily a good excited.

Kit rolled her eyes and gave Lord Starr half a smile. "What's wrong, Wolf?"

He came to a halt by the petting zoo fence and leaned on it to catch his breath. "DeepDelve...is opening three new Realms...and they're holding a draft to get in tonight!"

Lord Starr and Kit were agog, and soon all three were high-fiving and dancing in a circle.

When they finally stopped, Wolfgang gave Lord

Starr a playful shove. "You'll be in the first round, as top-ranked in this Realm."

Lord Starr shrugged, trying to repress his smile. "Yeah, but there's no guarantee someone will want me. Realm Owners usually don't want competition right out of the gate..."

"Yeah, OK. But if they pick you, you're in!" Wolfgang ran in place comically. "Dude, I heard the new Realms are, uh, there's a space one, and an island theme, and like a whole underwater world. You're bound to get into one of them. And then—BOOM! Starr Clan is born!"

"I don't know what Erin Hunter would have to say about that," Lord Starr joked. Wolfgang stared blankly back at him. "Ya know, Warriors? The cats, with the different clans—forget it."

Since the launch wasn't until that evening, Everett just logged out and got ready to go to his dad's. When he got back on about an hour later, an urgent notification was already waiting for him. Kit and Wolfgang jabbered at him over the in-game chat as they made their way toward his spawn point.

"Did you get an invite?"

"What Realm is it?"

"Can you bring a friend? Two friends?"

"What does it say?"

"Just give me a second!" he shouted, half-laughing. He scrolled through the message, trying to make sure he fully understood what it said.

"So...?"

"It says, 'Lord Starr, you are formally drafted into Antilla, the Island Realm...'"

Kit and Wolfgang cheered, as proud as if they had made it in themselves.

"'Should you accept the draft, your avatar will be reset and ported to Antilla—'"

"Reset?" Wolfgang blurted in his ear. "Like back to level one? No gear?"

"They don't want anyone to start the new Realm with an unfair advantage," Kit chimed in just as she rounded the corner of Lord Starr's manor. He was still busy looking over the Official Scroll.

Everett continued to read aloud. "'...at your earliest convenience, but cannot be delayed more than three (3) days.' Then it goes on to list a bunch of the rules unique to that Realm, some of the other draftees—"

Wolfgang reached them and trotted to a stop. "Ok, ok, that doesn't matter—can we come along?"

Lord Starr was silent for a long moment, prompting his friends to nudge him back to the present. Kit put a hand on his forearm as he continued to stare down. "Hey, you all right?"

"Can we come along?" Wolfgang pressed, but Kit shot him a look that wilted his smile.

Kit frowned up at Starr. "What's wrong?"

"The Realm Owner…"

"Yeah? Who is it?"

Lord Starr looked up at them both. "It's Jake."

The saga continues in Rip, The Realms Series Book 2!

Self-published authors depend on word of mouth to help reach new fans. Please consider leaving a review on Amazon, Goodreads, or both!

Acknowledgments:

My son, Andrew, for that unforgettable car ride where this whole crazy idea began.

My wife, Liz, for tolerating my hours at the computer, endlessly writing. For being my first critic, best editor, and biggest fan. I couldn't do any of this without your sincere, unwavering support.

To the many beta-readers who helped hammer this into a readable shape: Chris, Kelly, Jan, Regina, Richard, Kiyel, Rachel, and Charlie.

ABOUT THE AUTHOR

Matthew Lau was born and raised in York, Pennsylvania. He attended York College, Temple University, and Millersville University in his dual quest to become a writer and educator. He is now a middle school English teacher and the author of the dystopian novel <u>The Buried Few</u>. He lives with his wife and kids in Lancaster County, Pennsylvania.